Blade of the Poisoner

Douglas Hill was born in Canada, but has lived in London for some time. He has written non-fiction books on a variety of topics, edited science fiction anthologies, and until 1983 he was literary editor of the Labour weekly *Tribune*. His popular series of books for children are the *Last Legionary* quintet, featuring the intrepid Keill Randor, the *ColSec* trilogy and the *Huntsman* series.

The *Blade of the Poisoner* is an award-winning fantasy that marks an exciting departure for this highly acclaimed science fiction author.

D1147928

Douglas Hill

BLADE OF
THE POISONER

Piper Books

First published in Great Britain 1987 by Victor Gollancz Ltd
This Piper edition published 1989 by Pan Books Ltd,
Cavaye Place, London SW10 9PG
9 8 7 6 5 4 3 2 1
© Douglas Hill 1987
ISBN 0 330 30692 8

Printed and bound in Great Britain by
Richard Clay Ltd, Bungay, Suffolk

For Chris K.
in gratitude for many kinds of
moral support

and special thanks to Ken Adams,
fantasist, for the loan of his
expertise

CONTENTS

Part One

Gathering of Talents

Chapter 1

Death in the Wellwood

Jarral Gullen slid noiselessly forward through the brush. Gripping his spear firmly, he fixed his gaze on his quarry, feeding unaware in the sunlit glade. One more silent step forward . . . then one more. . . .

But an unseen briar, snagging his bare ankle, brought Jarral's game abruptly to a halt. "Ow!" he said, stumbling sideways. Three twigs snapped under his foot and a sapling threshed as he fell against it. His prey, a small, tufty-tailed rodent, swept up a tree with a volley of chittering abuse as Jarral's spear clattered harmlessly against a lower branch.

Jarral stepped out of the thicket, glanced up at the foliage where the little animal had disappeared, then gazed round at the great trees of the Wellwood, the forest that gave his village its name. The trees and shrubs still displayed the freshness of their early summer greening. Even the glade's carpeting of coarse grass was glowing with new green, dotted here and there with tiny wildflowers bright as jewels.

Jarral ambled across the glade to retrieve his weapon — a thin, slightly crooked stick that was a spear only in his imagination. Idly he used it to prod a small ant hill, then squatted to watch the insects scurry. He was just twelve years old, an ordinary boy from the tiny forest village. He was of average height and weight for his age, with plain brown hair and brown eyes and a plain, cheerful face, plainly dressed in shirt, breeches and sturdy shoes.

He glanced around the glade again. The day was wearing on towards mid-afternoon, and the overcast sky had begun to darken slightly as heavier clouds moved above the forest, bringing the murky threat of a thunderstorm. That did not trouble Jarral, for the weather was very often gloomy, with frequent swirls of storm clouds and mutters of thunder. In that land, sunlit days tended to be rare. But with the humid heaviness of the air, Jarral decided that what he wanted was a cool drink from the great spring-fed well on the fringe of the forest, around which clustered the villagers' cottages.

He set off at an easy jog towards the well. After his drink he supposed he should go and see if his cousins had any chores for him. He did not feel at all like doing chores, but he knew that his life would be a little more pleasant if he offered to do so, now and then.

The cousins, a quiet, elderly man and wife, had actually been cousins to Jarral's parents, who had died when he was an infant. The cousins had taken the boy in and had looked after him as well as they could. But they were a stolid pair with no children of their own. They filled their days with what seemed to be endless, plodding labour that was rarely lightened by affection or amusement. Because of them, and because there were no other children of Jarral's age in the tiny village, he had got quite used to his own company and to the games of his own invention in which he played the parts of warriors and heroes.

So, as he jogged through the shadow-patterns of the Wellwood and heard strange, faint noises in the distance, his imagination began at once to dream up a game, or a story, that might fit around those noises.

Then he stopped. A breeze had brought some of the sounds more clearly to his ears. They came from the direction of the village, now less than a mile away. And the half-invented game faded from his mind as uneasiness wrapped around him with a sudden chill.

The noises sounded like screams. Like the ragged screams of people gripped by unimaginable agony and terror.

He began to move forward again, tense and nervous, straining to hear more. Ahead, the land sloped steeply upwards towards a long, flat ridge that extended far into the distant forest depths. On much of the ridge an expanse of evergreens grew, leaving the ground free from dense brush. Jarral started up the slope, peering worriedly at the trees ahead. Then again he halted with a jolt, his heart leaping in a rush of panic.

Something had moved out from behind a tree near the top of the ridge. Something, or someone, huge and looming. . . .

Then recognition and relief filled Jarral's eyes. He half-raised a hand. "Archer!" he called, his voice cracking with relief.

The figure moved smoothly down the slope towards him, still huge but no longer threatening. Archer was a giant — twice Jarral's twelve-year-old height, half as tall again as the tallest man in the village. Archer was sun-browned and powerfully built, with arm muscles like cables from drawing the mighty bow that was slung across the broad shoulders.

But Archer also had a kindly face, bright grey eyes, dark brown curls, and a female shape within her jerkin and breeches of doeskin and her low, soft boots.

Archer had been visiting the village now and then for some years. She was a wandering hunter, with the huge bow that few men could draw — and with an uncanny skill that no man could match. During her visits she had always been especially kind to Jarral, claiming a fellowship since she had been raised an orphan, too, in her homeland far to the east. She had become one of Jarral's dearest friends —so that he had begun to dream that, one day, she might take him with her on her travels.

His dream was about to come true — though not in a way that Jarral could ever have imagined, or wished for.

His grin of greeting faded when he saw the look on Archer's usually cheerful face. A pain-filled darkness shadowed her broad brow, and anger flashed from her eyes and leaped in the clenched muscles of her jaw. For a moment Jarral thought that he had done something wrong. But then he saw that the giant woman's anger was not aimed at him. The village, he thought fearfully. She has come from the village.

"Archer, what's happening?" he asked.

Archer shook her head. "Horrible things, Jarral. Things I can hardly make myself speak about." Her grey eyes searched his, in a gaze that mingled sorrow and fury and deep distress. "You are young, Jarral, but you must be brave. What I must tell you will be the worst thing that you have known in your life."

Jarral stared, wide-eyed with fear.

Archer's mouth twisted. "The village has been destroyed, Jarral. Everyone is dead — except you. The cottages, the gardens, the barns and fields — all has been crushed and burned. There is nothing left."

The clouds above the forest rumbled with deep thunder as Archer spoke. Jarral had begun to shiver, seeing mental images of his cousins, his friends, the village as he knew it. Tears filled his eyes and a terrible coldness spread through him. Again his voice cracked slightly as he spoke. "Who . . . who did it? Why would anyone do that?"

Archer shook her head again. "I do not know why. But I know that the Prince Mephtik did it. Or ordered it to be done by his soldiers and his . . . creatures."

"Prince Mephtik?" Jarral had heard the name only once or twice before. Villagers mentioned it in nervous murmurs, if at all, and Jarral had known that it was a subject to be avoided.

"Mephtik, called the Poisoner," Archer said. "The ruler of all these lands, this whole eastern domain."

Jarral's trembling grew worse as tears blurred his vision. "Why would a prince destroy the village and . . . and kill everyone? What did we do?"

Archer laid a strong brown hand on his shoulder. "I do not know, Jarral. He is the Poisoner, a man of terrible cruelty and evil. He does many monstrous things that seem to have no meaning."

Jarral's tears finally spilled over. "What's going to happen to *me*?" he wailed.

"You will come with me," Archer said gently.

Jarral sobbed, then leaned forward against the towering figure. Archer put an arm around his shoulders, kindly and comforting as Jarral wept out his loss and bewilderment and fear. But in a moment, as the thunder growled again, Archer gripped his shoulders and stepped back.

"We cannot mourn properly now," she said. "The Poisoner's servants are still in the Wellwood. We must get away, swiftly."

"Can we go and . . . look at the village?" Jarral asked.

"No," Archer said quickly. "There is nothing left to see, except horror. Remember it as you last saw it. . . ."

Her voice broke off as she stiffened, then dropped into a low crouch, dragging Jarral down beside her. "Be still!" she hissed.

Panic clutched at Jarral again. "What . . . what . . . ?" he stammered.

"Soldiers," Archer said. "There."

Jarral's gaze followed her pointing finger, but even straining his eyes he could see no one. He was not surprised, for he had long known about Archer's astonishing keenness of eye over vast distances. But a second later he could just glimpse a movement, much farther along the ridge-top. It was a vague shape that looked like a horse and rider. And the rider seemed to be clad in something that was a weird, mottled green.

"Do the soldiers wear green?" Jarral asked.

As Archer nodded, an eerie sound came to their ears. Not distant thunder, this time, but a strange combination of a breathy hiss and a rapid, rustling patter, like the paws of two or three dogs galloping through the forest.

The sound turned Archer pale beneath her tan. She unslung her bow, drew from her quiver an arrow nearly as long as Jarral was tall, and gripped both so tensely that her arm muscles leaped and knotted.

"There is something besides soldiers on that ridge, Jarral," she murmured. "So now we must run, as fast as we can. You must keep going, deep into the forest, without looking back, without stopping. No matter what I do, or what you hear, keep running until you can run no more — and then walk or crawl if you must. But *do not stop*. Do you understand?"

Jarral was rigid with fright. On the distant ridge he saw another flicker of the mottled green of a soldier's uniform, then another. And beyond them, briefly visible in an open area, he seemed to see a weirdly shaped shadow, dark and low-slung, moving in what was surely an impossible way. . . .

A sob escaped his lips as he whirled and fled into the depths of the Wellwood, terror flinging him forward at a headlong speed, with Archer in a long-legged gallop just behind him.

Chapter 2

The Tainted Blade

Terror gathered around Jarral like a haze. It was as if he was flying along a narrow, leaf-walled tunnel. He saw only the twigs and thorns that clutched at him as he plunged through leafy tangles — only fallen logs or patches of bog that threatened to trip him up as he sped along the barely visible forest trail.

But his mind was half-aware of the eeriness around him — the ghastly silence among the trees. Even the thunder had faded, though dark clouds still shed murkiness on to the forest. It seemed as if every creature of the Wellwood, even the trees themselves, had been silenced by the presence of unnatural horror.

Then he stumbled and almost collapsed under a fresh assault of panic. He had realized he was alone. The steadying bulk of Archer was no longer behind him. Then he might have disobeyed the bow-woman's order — might have stopped running, turned to look back. But before he could do so he heard a series of noises in the distance.

One was the sound of galloping hooves, seeming very loud in that eerie stillness. As Jarral's pace faltered, he heard — from fairly close by — the deep, musical twang of Archer's bowstring. It was followed, from farther away, by a high-pitched human shriek — and an abrupt halt to the galloping hooves.

Then Archer was suddenly with him again, running

with long strides, not at all out of breath. "Do not slow down, Jarral!" she cried. "The danger is great!"

So Jarral resumed his desperate flight, ignoring the twinges in his leg muscles and the ache in his chest. Again the haze settled around him, blotting out everything but the tunnel-like trail ahead. And again, a few minutes later, Archer faded back, letting Jarral dash on alone.

This time, instead of hooves in the distance, he heard that other combination of sounds, the weird hissing and pattering. The memory of that dimly glimpsed shadow on the ridge sent a shock-wave of icy terror along his spine, which poured new energy into his tiring legs. Once again Archer's bowstring sang its baritone note. But the sound of pursuit did not stop. The fearsome hiss and patter kept on — only slowly seeming to swing aside and fade away.

Could Archer have *missed*? The thought nearly drove Jarral to his knees, for she had never done so in all the times he had seen her shoot. Then Archer was at his side again, running tirelessly, but with a grim and troubled expression, indicating that Jarral's thoughts had been correct.

But at least the arrow must have driven the unknown horror off their trail, for they ran on now surrounded only by the ominous stillness. By that time, Jarral's legs were like lifeless wood and his lungs were aflame. But still Archer urged him on, still his panic drove him like a whip. Eyes blurred with near-exhaustion as well as fear, he did not see the barrier across the trail. Not until Archer, with a cry, clamped a great hand on the back of his shirt and flung him sideways into a leafy bush.

There he lay for a moment, breathing in huge sobbing gulps, before crawling slowly out of the bush. And fresh terror closed round his throat and body like huge cold fingers.

The barrier was like a large net, with a loosely woven pattern made from silvery cords that gleamed as if covered in wetness. The pattern extended across the trail from one tall tree to another, reaching upwards higher than Archer's head.

It took Jarral several seconds to recognize the barrier, though he had seen others like it many times. The others had been . . . far smaller.

The barrier was a web. An enormous, sticky spider's web.

Jarral struggled to his feet, backing away white-faced from the monstrous web. Within two paces he collided with Archer, behind him, who seemed to be standing very still. Slowly Jarral turned — and froze.

He was looking at a squad of soldiers, all in the uniforms of unpleasantly mottled green, like a reptile's hide. From the backs of their necks armoured collars rose, looking as solid as metal, curving up and over their heads to form helmets like ugly serpentine hoods. The soldiers all held heavy crossbows, aimed unwaveringly at Archer. And behind them . . . Jarral's knees went watery at the glimpse of the shape in the shadows.

Its bulbous body, like a bristly dark sack, was the size of a large dog — and was supported by eight long, springy, jointed legs. Several eyes glittered redly from the head, while below those eyes, curved jaws like huge fangs slowly opened and closed.

For a long moment they all stood motionless, the soldiers staring cold-eyed at their captives. Then the soldiers moved smartly aside as past them stalked a tall, narrow man with long white hair and a short black beard. His hair was held back by an emerald-studded coronet of silver, and more emeralds and silver decorated the dark-green leather of his long tunic. From a broad silver belt around his waist hung a silver sheath out of which jutted the hilt of a short sword — a hilt that seemed to be carved from a single huge emerald.

The man's close-set eyes surveyed Archer and Jarral disdainfully. Then he smiled, showing sharp and unpleasantly stained teeth.

"An excellent hunt." His voice was slightly high-pitched, with a discordant edge that made Jarral's skin crawl. "How amusing to see again that frightened beasts will flee blindly into traps."

Archer ignored him, staring watchfully at the group of soldiers. The man's smile faded and his dark brows fell in a glower.

"She has not been disarmed," he snapped.

"No, Highness," said one of the soldiers quickly. His helmet and sleeve held badges that looked like insignia of command. "Your pardon, Highness." He stepped forward, gesturing with his crossbow at Archer. "Throw down your bow, and the knife at your belt!"

For a long moment Archer did not move. Her gaze seemed to grow even more piercing, so that the officer blinked and almost quailed. But then he raised the crossbow, finger taut on the release. Archer glanced at Jarral, grimaced as if in apology, and flung her weapons to the ground.

The white-haired man was still glowering. "Nor has she been bound," he snarled.

"Your pardon, Highness," said the officer again, nervously. But before he could move, the white-haired man raised a narrow hand.

"It seems I must do these things myself," he said peevishly. Turning, he made a complex series of gestures, a pattern in the air. And Jarral was unable to hold back a yelp of fear.

The eight-legged horror had surged forward out of the shadows, in a pattering scuttle of terrifying speed. As it approached, it flung out from its body a length of the same glistening cord that formed the web. The cord hissed through the air to wrap itself around Archer's upper body before the giant woman could begin to avoid it.

Archer strained every great muscle, but the cord did not yield. Jarral saw that it was as sticky as any spider-web, clinging tightly to Archer's jerkin and skin. Then the monster retreated at another signal from the white-haired man, who was smiling with satisfaction.

"Excellent," he said. "A most gratifying day. All shall be rewarded."

"Thank you, Highness," said the officer, bowing his head with a vivid expression of relief, which was reflected on the faces of his men.

"Now, giantess," the white-haired man went on. "Explain your presence here."

Archer took a deep breath. "We are but innocent wayfarers, Prince Mephtik," she said. The name jolted Jarral, even though he had guessed by then who their captor must be.

Mephtik gave a snarling laugh. "Innocent you probably never were — and certainly not now that you have slain one of my men. Your arrows fly too far, and too true, for those of a mere wayfarer." The ugly laugh became a cackle. "I'm quite sure I *know* what you and the whelp are — and I will soon have it confirmed by my Master."

Jarral had no idea what he meant. But something in Mephtik's voice, and an answering deep flicker of tension in Archer's eyes, brought out an icy sweat on Jarral's skin.

"The boy, I believe," Mephtik was saying, "is a survivor from that wretched village. And you, giantess, are almost certainly an agent of that fool of a wizard who dreams of opposing my Master."

"Whatever I may be, Prince," Archer said calmly, "the boy is of no importance. Do with me what you choose, but release him."

"Do you give me orders?" Mephtik raised a mocking eyebrow, then snickered. "No, no, I shall do with *both* as I choose. A person of your size and strength, giantess, will provide a valuable subject on whom I can test some of my newer venoms." He laughed again. "I can guarantee you many weeks of unbridled torment before I finally put an end to you."

Then Jarral flinched as Mephtik turned cold eyes towards him.

"As for the whelp, he is merely a piece of unfinished business. But it would be a pity to finish it too soon. His pathetic village was erased far too quickly to provide much amusement." His grin was demonic. "Perhaps the boy should be honoured — through being shown the way to death by my favourite plaything."

His narrow hand reached down, drawing the short, emerald-hilted sword from its sheath. Jarral stared at it, paralyzed, like a bird hypnotized by a snake. The sword's silvery blade was *stained*, all along its gleaming length. And the stain was another shade of Mephtik's favourite colour — a livid, sickly green.

Bound as she was, Archer flung herself in front of Jarral. "Mephtik, you cannot!" she shouted. "He is a *child*! Use your vile Blade on me if it must be used!"

"I have told you of my plans for you, outlaw," Mephtik said coldly. At his gesture, soldiers dragged

Archer roughly aside. Two others gripped Jarral, immovably. As Mephtik raised the stained sword, grinning when Jarral tried to cringe away, one of the soldiers pulled open the front of Jarral's shirt, baring his chest.

"Let me tell you about my toy," Mephtik said to Jarral. A redness had appeared in the prince's cheeks, a cruel glitter in his eyes. "It is a gift to me from my Master — a weapon of great and special power. A *magical* sword, boy. People call it — the Tainted Blade."

He swept the sword-tip past Jarral's face and cackled as the boy cowered back.

"But I prefer another name," he went on. "I call it the Blade of Lingering Death. *Lingering*, boy — note that. A mere scratch from this Blade will be fatal. But not at once. In fact, *not until the next full turning of the moon*. And then the person with the scratch falls dead as if stabbed to the heart. Do you understand? No ill effects at all, until the moon completes its changes — and then, instant death!"

Again he brandished the Blade, again he laughed his cruel laugh.

"But *during* that time, before the moon changes . . ." he went on. "Think of it! In every moment of every day, the wounded person sees his death drawing closer, reaching for him. In every moment, for all those days, he feels terror and despair, waiting for the moon to complete its changes. He is *dying*, in his mind, all that time. Dying in every moment of every day. . . ."

Mephtik's voice had become shrill, and a small fleck of foam had appeared at one corner of his mouth. With an effort he gathered himself, and stared at Jarral with burning eyes.

"Here is your honour, boy," he snarled. "Last night the moon was full. Four weeks hence another full moon will rise, though you will not see it. By then you will be in my throne room, to provide my entertainment, but you will not enjoy it. For that full moonrise will be the last moment of your life." He tittered evilly. "Take my mark, boy — and begin your month of dying!"

The Tainted Blade reached out towards Jarral's bare chest. But then it halted. Mephtik, startled, seemed to strain every lean muscle of his arm to force the sword to move. But it did not budge. Then the Poisoner's eyes widened and sweat burst from his brow. The Blade had begun to swing *away* from Jarral. Shakily but steadily, its deadly point rose, then began to curve backwards.

Within a moment, despite the Poisoner's frantic efforts, the lethal Blade in his hand was pointing towards his own throat.

Staring wildly around, Mephtik saw Archer. Still bound by the spider's cord, she seemed to be under incredible tension — every muscle of jaw, neck and shoulder taut and bulging. And her luminous grey eyes were fixed on the Blade in the Poisoner's hand, as it inched towards his throat.

"It's a *Talent*!" Mephtik screeched. "Stop her! *Stop her!*"

The soldiers seemed frozen with shock, gaping at the moving Blade. But then their officer lunged forward, swinging the crossbow like a club. Archer crumpled to the ground, sudden blood staining her brown curls. And the unseen force that had gripped the Blade vanished, so that the weapon jerked violently in Mephtik's hand.

Then the Poisoner gathered himself, glaring furiously at Jarral. "So you see there is no escape, for you or her," he snarled. "Now begins your death — which will end finally when next the moon is full."

Again he reached out with the Tainted Blade, this time with nothing to impede him. The sickly green tip of the Blade touched Jarral's chest, cold as a shard of ice. A thin line of red appeared on the skin as the Blade-tip moved. Slowly, skilfully, Mephtik drew the Blade up and down, up and down again.

The surgically neat cut — just skin-deep — traced on Jarral's chest, in his blood, a perfect letter M.

But Jarral was unaware of the shape of the cut. The mounting series of horrors that had assailed him finally proved overwhelming. Mephtik's words and the first icy touch of the Tainted Blade had flashed through his entire being in a crushing wave of shock. Before his wound had fully begun to bleed, he had sagged in the grip of his captors, his mind spiralling down into a welcome, pain-free darkness.

Chapter 3

Many Blades

Earlier, many days and nights before Jarral was to feel the icy touch of the Tainted Blade — and many days' march to the west of the Wellwood — a crowd had gathered in one street of a mighty city. The city was Xicanti, the capital where Prince Mephtik had his Stronghold. But the street where the crowd had gathered lay in another part of the city, a poor and decrepit area. And the crowd itself was ill-clad and uncouth — as rough as the bare wooden planks that formed the platform around which they clustered.

Night was well advanced in the city, so the platform was lit by the flame of torches, shedding their orange gleam on the eyes and sweaty faces of the crowd as they grinned or yelled. On the platform, a troupe of travelling entertainers had been performing for about an hour — and receiving plenty of noisy appreciation.

But the person on stage at that moment had almost managed to silence the crowd. He was a man slightly below average height, with a shock of short dark hair, wearing only a dark loincloth and knee-high boots. His lean body was pale and hairless, slabbed with muscle as hard and sharply defined as a sculpture.

He was a juggler, but this was no ordinary juggling of balls or hoops or light clubs. A brightly lettered sign at one side of the stage announced: CARVER — MAN OF MANY BLADES. And several of those blades were spinning in the air above him.

What had almost silenced the crowd was that all those blades were slim, needle-pointed poniards and stilettos. Each one was whirling through two neat turns above the juggler's head before he caught it by the hilt to spin it up again. The action looked easy, almost casual, although the man's eyes seemed narrowed with concentration, glittering almost wolfishly through slitted lids.

The only part of the crowd that did not hold its breath while the blades spun was a foursome of bulky, half-drunk men, wearing uniforms of mottled green with armoured collars rising like serpentine hoods. Those men preferred to hoot and bellow, as if trying to break the juggler's concentration, as if hoping that one of the daggers hurled high into the night would plunge down to more dire effect.

But it did not happen. Within a few moments, the juggler was gathering in his blades, nodding briefly as the crowd roared its applause. The roars became more tumultuous when the juggler was joined on stage by a smiling young woman, whose shapely figure was barely covered by a sleeveless top and a semi-transparent skirt.

The four soldiers made the most noise when she appeared, with some bellowed remarks that were more coarse than even that rowdy company could enjoy. But no one objected. The four men were big and well-armed — and everyone knew who their master was.

As for the juggler, he seemed indifferent to all the noise, merely standing quietly to one side next to an oddly shaped sack of coarse cloth. When the young woman could make herself heard, she cheerily announced the finale of the entertainment.

"The Man of Many Blades will now demonstrate his skill at *throwing* those blades! Knives, axes, short swords

— he is master of them all! And he will throw at a living target — myself!"

With a flourish she swept off the skirt, showing that her top was part of a skimpy one-piece costume. The crowd roared again, with more crude bellows from the four soldiers. Then the young woman strutted over to some upright planks at one side of the stage, painted a smeared off-white. Placing her back against those planks, she waited, smiling, as the juggler began to take an assortment of bladed weapons from the sack next to him. As the young woman had promised, they came in every sort — more stilettos, many hunting knives, skinning knives, heavy dirks, one short sword, several hatchets and two narrow, beautifully balanced throwing knives.

The young woman held up her hands for silence. "In this final act, Carver will perform as no other knifeman in the world would dare perform!" She paused dramatically as the audience gawped. "He will throw these weapons — at *me*, remember — while *blindfolded*!"

The crowd stared, open-mouthed, as the man called Carver drew from the sack a band of soft leather and fastened it around his eyes.

One of the soldiers hooted scornfully. "'S a trick!" he yelled. "Fakery!"

"Course it's a trick, dolt," said the biggest of the four, who was their sergeant. "And we'll prove it to these clowns before he's done!"

The others grinned and settled back to watch. The juggler had begun to pick up the weapons, one by one, whirling them up into the air in another intricate juggling pattern. His blindfolded head seemed to be turned slightly away, so that he was facing the stained dark curtains at the back of the stage rather than his female target. Within moments, all the weapons were spinning and glinting through the torchlit air. The crowd was holding its breath in near-silence as the juggler's lean hands kept up the pattern without effort.

By then a few more voices were beginning to echo the soldier's shout, that it was all a trick — for who could juggle anything, let alone so many blades, with his eyes covered? But most of the crowd was untroubled. If it was a trick, it was an intensely entertaining trick.

Then, collectively, the crowd jerked and gasped. Out of the midst of the juggling pattern, one of the blades had been thrown. It was the short sword, flashing across the stage to bury its point in the planking a finger's-breadth above the young woman's glossy hair.

She grinned, the crowd whooped with delight, and the juggler calmly continued. Regularly, smoothly, with one hand and then the other, he sent weapon after weapon whirling out of the juggling pattern. One after another sank with a vibrating thud into the whitened planks. Slowly they began to outline the young woman's body. One of the dirks bit into the wood close enough to touch the cloth at her waist, but her brave grin did not flinch. One of the hatchets slammed into a plank only a hair's thickness from her thigh, but not a muscle in the bare leg moved.

At last she was almost fully outlined by weaponry jutting from the planks. The man called Carver was left with only the two wicked-looking throwing knives, one in each hand. With a snap of his wrists he flung them both high above the stage into the darkness. Again the crowd held its breath, seeing that he had not moved his head, that he was still holding his blindfolded face turned slightly to one side.

The two knives plummeted back down into the torch-light — and the juggler smoothly plucked them from the air by their hilts, one in each hand, and hurled them. An instant later, they were both quivering in the planking, one on either side of the young woman's throat, nestling against her skin.

For that instant the audience was totally silenced, staring with wonderment and, in some cases, a tinge of fear. As the juggler walked over to the young woman to collect his weapons, the onlookers seemed to be asking themselves — *was* it a trick? And if it was not — how could it be possible?

Then the awed stillness was shattered by a bellow from the green-clad sergeant, lunging to his feet. "Run out of blades, *blind* man?" he roared. "Have mine!"

And he snatched a heavy knife from his belt and threw it.

It was thrown with some skill and considerable power, and it was aimed for the dead centre of the juggler's back. But no one in the crowd had time even to register shock at the murderous attack when a greater shock struck them.

The juggler, still blindfolded, with his back to the crowd, had not reacted in any way to the sergeant's roar. But in the last fraction of an instant, as the knife flashed towards him, he twisted his lean body to one side. The knife flew past his shoulder, driving into a plank.

And even as the sergeant's jaw was beginning to drop with amazement, the juggler jerked the knife from the wood, spun and hurled it back. With unnerving accuracy it flew above the heads of the crowd to strike deep into the wooden table where the soldiers were sitting. By reflex they jerked away, tipping over their chairs and the table that held their drinks, sprawling on the floor, drenched in a cascade of ale.

As the juggler plucked the two throwing knives from the planking and strode off-stage, the crowd erupted into riotous cheering — mingled with uproarious laughter at the stunned, ale-soaked sergeant and his men.

The curtains at the back of the stage led into a narrow shed where some small dressing rooms had been set up, with leather hangings at the door. The juggler stalked into one of the rooms, which was lit by another flickering torch, and tossed the two knives on to a crude table that held a small scratched mirror. Removing the strip of leather from his eyes, he tossed that beside the knives — before turning, eyes slitted, to the doorway at the sound of a soft knock.

The young woman from the stage came in, carrying the clanking sack of his bladed weapons. Setting it on the floor, she looked at him with concern.

"You took a great risk with the soldiers," she said quietly.

His eyes flashed orange in the torchlight. "*They* took the risk, Dorinna," he said with a thin smile.

"They're soldiers of the Poisoner," the young woman told him, frowning. "And you've made enemies of them."

"I've had worse enemies," the juggler said.

"I don't doubt that," Dorinna replied. For a moment she gazed at him, nibbling her lip. "Carver — won't you tell me?" she finally burst out. "How you *do* it? *I* know it's a real blindfold — and that sergeant's knife was thrown at your *back*!"

The man called Carver shrugged. "I've told you, Dorinna. I have a . . . trick, for seeing past the blindfold. But it's my stage secret. As for that lout's knife, I was lucky. That's all."

Dorinna looked at him sadly. "Why is it that I don't believe you?" she asked. And she turned swiftly and went out.

The juggler sighed wearily. Then, as if putting Dorinna out of his mind, he picked up the sack of weapons and took it to the far corner where there stood a tall, curious staff of dark wood. It was about the juggler's height, oddly carved for a short distance at the upper end, with a thong that would allow it to be slung over a shoulder. And it was slightly curved, for more than half its length.

But the juggler ignored the staff. Crossing back to the table with the smeared mirror, he picked up a small satchel from beneath it. Out of the satchel he took some items of clothing and pulled them on — loose trousers that tucked into his boots, a dark shirt with cuffs tight at the wrists. Then, without looking in the mirror, he put his fingertips to each eye in succession, and removed from beneath his eyelids two small curved pieces of glass. On each piece there was *painted* the appearance of an eye, complete with iris and pupil. The painting had been done with almost magical skill, amazingly life-like.

But the juggler's own eyes, now exposed, were eerily, inhumanly lifeless — two surfaces of cold and shiny black.

Carefully the juggler placed the bits of glass on the table, next to the throwing knives and the leather blindfold. Then, reaching again towards the satchel, he paused. Something strange had begun to happen to the mirror at his side.

It had begun to reveal an image — at first only a series of orange streaks, like reflections of the torch's flame. But at once the streaks settled, shifting themselves slowly into letters, a group of words.

The man named Carver stiffened, motionless and alert. Yet, oddly, he still did not turn to *look* at the mirror as the message formed:

**SEEK ARCHER IN THE WELLWOOD
SAVE THE BOY**

Chapter 4

Departure

After a moment the letters began to fade, until once again the face of the mirror was blank. And still the juggler had not moved, except for the grimace that briefly twisted his mouth.

"Wouldn't bother to mention where to *find* a Wellwood," he muttered to himself. "Or why Archer can't save the boy — whoever he is."

He picked up the satchel and began to remove its contents — mostly spare clothing, including a cloak of a blue so dark as to be almost black. After examining each item he repacked them all carefully, except for the cloak, which he tossed on to the table. Then he went over to the sack that held his weapons and took from it a heavy dirk, sheathed, with a blade nearly as long as his forearm. That, too, he took back to the table, where for a moment he paused, as if pondering.

"This will make Dorinna unhappy," he muttered. Then a wry smile twitched the corners of his mouth. "For about a day and a half."

And that was the moment when the leather hangings on the doorway were abruptly ripped aside.

Through the opening lunged the green-uniformed sergeant and his three men, swords ready in their hands.

The man called Carver did not start or flinch or even blink. He merely shifted his feet slightly as if to improve his balance and stood still, waiting.

The sergeant gestured with his sword. "All right, *blind man*," he growled. "You're gonna learn you can't make a fool out of *me*!"

The juggler's mouth twitched. "You're doing that all by yourself," he said coolly.

The sergeant flushed dark with rage, roared and swung his sword in a furious arc. If the blow had landed, the juggler's head would have rolled on the floor. But the juggler had moved, a darting leap almost too swift to follow. The other three soldiers had only just registered the fact that their sergeant's sword had missed when the juggler slammed in among them. Though he was shorter and slimmer than any one of them, the three were flung staggering aside, like scattered bowling pins. One tumbled to the floor, one thumped against the wall, the third crashed noisily into the table with the mirror.

The juggler's foot flashed out twice in well-aimed kicks, and two of the soldiers shrieked and folded in the middle, clutching themselves. But as the juggler turned towards the third soldier, coming away from the wrecked table, the sergeant attacked again, his sword stabbing viciously at the juggler's back.

As before, on the stage, the juggler seemed to be aware of the attack from behind. He swayed smoothly aside, just in time. The sergeant's sword flashed past him to bite deep into the sword-arm of the third soldier.

In that instant the juggler was leaping for the curved staff in the far corner. As his hand found it, the wounded soldier was howling, the sergeant was bellowing — and through the doorway stepped young Dorinna, who took one look at the mêlée and screamed.

In the midst of that din, the juggler's hand gripped the carved top of the staff, twisted it and pulled. With a faint click the top came loose — showing itself to be the carved hilt of a sword, which slid smoothly out of the staff. It was a long, slim, bright sword, with a slightly curved blade that looked lethally sharp.

But that sword faced no opposition. The three soldiers were slumped on the floor, moaning. Dorinna had stumbled back against the door-frame, eyes round with fear. And the sergeant was standing very still and staring with bulging eyes at the juggler.

Clearly in the heat of battle the sergeant had not looked too closely at his opponent. But now, in that tiny pause, he had looked. And he had seen the curved sword, and the glittering blackness of the juggler's eyes.

Sweating and shaken, the sergeant let his sword dangle from his almost nerveless hand. "Your eyes . . ." he breathed.

The words directed the attention of Dorinna to the same place. With a choked version of her previous scream, she slid bonelessly to the floor in a dead faint.

"I've . . . heard of one like you," the sergeant was saying. He began edging back towards the door, his voice ragged. "A warrior with great skill . . . whose dead black eyes can see behind and before, all around, in every direction."

"You've heard that, have you?" the juggler said, almost idly.

"Men say he may be a demon, or a Talent," the sergeant went on shakily. He had nearly reached the door. "They say his true name rises from the curved blade he wields. Scythe, they call him. Scythe the blind man . . . Scythe the Seer."

"You shouldn't worry about names too much," the juggler said calmly.

But the sergeant was still staring at the curved sword glinting in the torchlight. Just as bright, just as cold, the light flashed from the shiny black eyes of the man called Carver, the man named Scythe.

"Scythe the Seer . . ." the sergeant choked, his face twisting. "Scythe the Slayer. . . ."

And he whirled and sprang through the door, in a burst of speed born of terror.

Scythe jerked forward as if he might pursue, but then drew back. Smiling his small chill smile, he turned towards the wounded soldier, now half-unconscious from loss of blood. Scythe could see — without needing to turn his head — that the other two soldiers had mostly recovered. But they remained on the floor, weapons forgotten, staring up at him. One of them whimpered as Scythe stood over the wounded man, his curved sword sweeping down.

But the incredible keenness of the blade merely sliced a strip of cloth from the man's uniform, with which Scythe bound up the slashed arm.

"I might have killed your sergeant, had he stayed to fight," he said conversationally to the other two, who were still staring at him as mice stare at a hunting cat. "But I don't kill those who are unarmed or unconscious — or unmanned with fear."

Then he turned away, ignoring them as he slid the curved sword back into the staff. Moving to the shattered table, he halted, muscles clenching in his jaw. Everything that had been on the table had been spilled on to the floor. And the two small pieces of painted glass, which he had worn over his eyes, had been crushed to powder by a soldier's boot.

"At least they deceived Dorinna these months," he

murmured to himself. "So now I must be a blind beggar again."

He picked up the strip of leather and fastened it over his eyes, then took up the two throwing knives and the heavy dirk. The dirk's sheath went on to his belt at one hip, while the knives slid into sheaths within his shirt, at the back of his collar. Then he gathered up the dark-blue cloak, slung it and the satchel over a shoulder, grasped the staff and strode towards the door. But there he paused, gazing down at the still unconscious form of Dorinna. Sighing, he slung the staff's thong over his other shoulder, then stooped and without apparent effort lifted Dorinna's limp form from the floor, before vanishing through the door.

For a long moment there was silence in the room. Then the two uninjured soldiers expelled long, shaky breaths and began to climb to their feet, wincing slightly.

"What d'we do now?" one said.

The other shrugged. "Go find th' serg'nt, I reckon."

"He'll still be runnin'," the first soldier said with a grimace. "An' me too, if I was him. I never faced *nobody* like that."

His comrade nodded. "Got to be some kind of devil-spawn, eyes like that. Got to be no kind of *human* . . ."

He broke off as if his throat had suddenly closed, staring at the doorway.

The cloaked figure with the headband and the staff had silently reappeared, as if sprouting from the floor. He had obviously placed Dorinna safely somewhere, and just as obviously had heard what the soldiers had been saying.

"I'm human," Scythe said easily, his chill smile flickering. "If I'm cut, I bleed." The smile vanished. "But you two together will never be good enough to find that out for yourselves."

The soldiers gulped and flinched.

"I don't suppose," Scythe went on, "that either of you knows a place called the Wellwood?"

They glanced at each other and gulped again. "Yessir," one said shakily. "Wellwood, sir. Big forest, a long ways east, sir. Beyond the Far Barrens. You follow the Bloodvein River, turn north-east past a big waterfall called the Chimes. Sir."

"Good," Scythe said. "I know the Barrens." He frowned slightly. "But how is it you know the route so well?"

"All of us know it now," the soldier said, his voice still shaky. "The Prince Mephtik, he's travellin' out that way. To go . . . huntin'."

Scythe's mouth went thin as a sword-slash. "Hunting. Now I understand. I know very well what happens when the Poisoner *hunts*."

He stood silent for a moment, as the soldiers quailed back from the steely anger that showed on his face. Then the dark cloak swirled, and the two men were once again staring at an empty doorway.

Chapter 5

Meeting of Minds

Some days later, Scythe rode slowly along a dusty road far to the east of the city where he had performed as a juggler. He seemed to sag in the saddle as he rode, as if overcome by weariness and gloom. The dark-blue cloak hung limply down, hiding the dirk and half-covering the staff that was slung beside the saddle. The cloak was travel-stained, the band around his eyes was sweat-stained, his face was grimy with dust. Even his mount looked miserable — a gangling, bony horse of a dull muddy-brown colour, whose head drooped as its rider's did.

All in all, Scythe looked like a sightless, poverty-stricken, wretched wanderer — which is just how he wished to look. There were many such folk in Prince Mephtik's realm, homeless and hopeless drifters, staying alive through odd jobs or petty crime or begging. They were sometimes sneered at and abused, sometimes pitied and given a coin or two, most often ignored. Scythe wanted very much to be ignored.

The road — little more than a vague trail — led through an expanse of wild country, where the thin soil showed a great many sharp grey outcrops of rock and many fewer tufts of coarse grass or scrubby patches of trees. This was the Far Barrens, where the land rose and fell in a series of low ridges and shallow dips. And the road kept itself cautiously winding among the dips and gullies, so that a traveller would never be framed against the sky. That sky was overcast, as usual, with streaks of darker cloud running among the grey, and occasional faint mumbles of thunder.

In the near distance, on Scythe's left, the silty waters of the Bloodvein River drifted by. And ahead, farther to the east, Scythe could just hear a sound that might have been more thunder rumbling, except that it was continuous.

"That's it, Hob," he said to the horse. "The waterfall. We'll camp there tonight and take our bearings."

The bony horse had swivelled an ear back towards him as he spoke. But then both its ears switched forward as it jerked up its head.

Scythe had also spotted the movement ahead of them. Above the road, on the crest of a small ridge, a rider had appeared. The horse seemed light in colour, perhaps white, and the rider seemed fairly small. But even Scythe's uncanny vision could make out no more detail at that distance. The rider seemed to pause, as if watching Scythe — or perhaps waiting.

"Not wearing green, anyway, whoever it is," Scythe muttered. He shook the reins, urging Hob out of his loose-jointed plod into an easy trot.

In almost the same instant, Scythe stiffened. Behind him, coming into view around a bend in the road, he saw — without turning — a group of seven riders. And these *were* wearing green. The soldiers saw Scythe at the same time and kicked their horses forward.

"Getting crowded here," Scythe said, shaking the reins again. "*Run*, Hob!"

The horse surged forward — and instantly its bony, ungainly appearance was shown to be deceptive. Hob seemed to flow along the ground in an effortless, distance-devouring stride. Ahead, Scythe saw that the unknown rider's pale horse had also broken into a gallop, down the slope of the ridge. But then the rider swung the horse to one side, vanishing into an expanse of trees and scrub brush.

"To the woods," Scythe muttered. "Good idea."

Hob's storming gallop soon brought him to the same stand of woods. Behind, Scythe could see the dust cloud raised by his pursuers, but for a moment the soldiers were hidden by another curve in the road. With a touch of a knee Scythe sent Hob into a surefooted swerve towards the trees. There he gripped the staff and leaped from the saddle, landing on his feet and taking a few running steps, as balanced as an acrobat.

"*On*, Hob!" he shouted. And as the horse thundered away through the trees, Scythe drew his curved sword from the staff and sprang for a nearby thicket. Dropping the staff and cloak, drawing the dirk for his other hand, he waited for the seven soldiers.

Soon he heard their horses out on the road, but the sounds indicated that they were riding past. He began to edge forward out of the thicket, knowing that the soldiers would soon realize what had happened and would come back to search the woods. But then he froze.

Clearly visible to his unique vision, someone was creeping silently through the trees behind him.

It was a young girl, slim, blonde and pretty, despite a slightly superior expression around her pert mouth. She wore a fine lacy shirt under a long riding tunic of dusky red, tight leggings of the same colour and high black boots — with the ivory hilt of a narrow dagger at her waist. Her clothing was made of rich material, expensively decorated, as were the saddle and harness and travelling bag on the beautiful creamy-white mare she was leading.

She did not seem to have spotted Scythe, crouched in the brush, but he did not wait to be discovered.

"Stop where you are, girl," he snapped, rising and turning.

The girl's face went chalk-white. She had seen him turn to face her only after he began to speak. And then she had seen the band across his eyes. "How . . . how did you see . . . ?" she asked.

Scythe shook his head. "The question is why you're coming up behind me."

The girl was still shocked, but a flash of haughty anger showed in her eyes. "I didn't even *see* you. I was watching for the soldiers."

Scythe studied her for a moment, then nodded. "Then what," he asked, "is a little rich girl doing out here alone, hiding from soldiers?"

The girl drew herself up. "You will not speak to me so! I am the Lady Mandragorina, daughter of Lord Felley of Felley Hale, who is Warden of the northern region."

Scythe shrugged. "If you say so. The question still stands. Why are you here?"

Her glare faded a little as she seemed to grow ill at ease. "I was . . . *sent* to this road, to wait for someone." Her uneasiness increased. "I was told to seek a . . . a blind man who sees more fully than men with eyes." She was watching Scythe, looking more flustered as he began to smile. "You cover your eyes, yet you seemed to see me behind you. . . ."

Scythe's wry smile widened slightly. "By any chance," he said, "were you sent by one who wears only blue, has a

44

very good opinion of himself and likes speaking in riddles?"

Mandragorina's relieved smile was like the sun after rain. "Oh, yes — that's Cryl."

Scythe nodded. "Cryltaur Tabbetang — sorcerer, outlaw, humorist, collector of Talents . . . who could never do anything so simple as tell you my name."

Her giggle was silvery music. "Still, I suppose there can be no other blind man with vision, like you. It must be a true Talent, of course?"

Scythe nodded. "I can see all around me, above and below, all at once. But with part of my mind, not my eyes." He reached up and pulled the leather band away.

"Oh," she said in a small voice, staring at the shiny blackness within his eye-sockets. "The grim reaper. . . ."

Scythe looked startled. "Why do you say that?"

"An image came to my mind," she said uneasily. "Of a figure in a hooded cloak, bearing a scythe."

He nodded dourly as he replaced the headband. "I've had many names in many places, but most often — by those who know me — I'm called Scythe. Because like the figure in your image I've harvested a number of lives — from the camp of the Enemy. And will harvest a few more before my time is done." He smiled his chill smile. "And that is *your* Talent, then, that brought you to Cryl? Reaching into the minds of others?"

"In a way," Mandragorina said. "But getting images *from* other minds happens only with some difficulty. My *main* Talent. . . ."

She stopped, tensing, at Scythe's abrupt silencing gesture. From the edge of the woods came the muffled thump of hooves, the rattle of harness. The seven soldiers had returned.

"Where is your horse?" Mandragorina whispered.

"I sent him on," Scythe told her softly. "The green ones would find a cat in these woods more easily than my Hob, if he's hiding. But with you and your mare, we have little chance of staying out of sight."

"You're wrong," she said briskly. "With me there is *every* chance."

But Scythe was paying no attention. Still gripping his two weapons, he jerked his head at Mandragorina and began to move stealthily away.

"Stay *here*!" she hissed sharply. "Just stand still and don't make a *sound*!"

Scythe turned, frowning — but then froze into a half-crouch. His vision showed him, to one side, three green-clad riders, with crossbows ready, moving slowly through the brush.

At the same moment when the three men swung their gaze towards the man and the girl standing with the white mare, Mandragorina went strangely tense — eyes closed, mouth pursed, a frown drawing down her pale brows.

The soldiers' gaze swept over them — and past. They did not blink or change expression. Their mounts whickered and shook their heads as if suddenly fretful, but the soldiers merely jerked at the reins and moved steadily forward. One came within a hand's-breadth of the astonished Scythe but did not look at him, merely peering briefly at the nearby thicket. Then the men moved on, deeper into the woods.

A silent moment later, a voice shouted from somewhere in the brush. "Nothin'! He musta ridden out on the far side!" Then there was a thudding of hooves, fading slowly.

Scythe released the breath he had been holding. "That was well done — whatever it was."

Mandragorina's smile held a touch of pride. "My main Talent is in making people see things, or not. They looked at us and saw three small bushes."

"Their horses seemed troubled," Scythe said.

"The horses *saw* what the men saw," she replied. "But they could smell us — especially Pearl, my mare. We must have seemed very strange bushes to them."

Scythe inclined his head. "Then my thanks — and apologies for not paying attention, at first." His thin smile twitched. "A pleasure to meet you, my lady Mandragorina. I hope we can be friends as well as allies in the service of that riddling wizard."

"My friends call me Mandra," she said with an answering smile.

"Mandra it is," Scythe said. "And that" — he pointed to the ungainly shape of his horse, who had ambled into view — "that is my faithful Hob, whose name comes from Hobgoblin, or Hobby-horse, or Hobbledehoy, depending on my mood. He's not as lovely as your Pearl, but he has surprised many men and outrun many horses. In times past he has been my only friend."

As he was speaking, the muddy-brown horse had nickered in a friendly way at the pretty mare, whose eyes gleamed with interest. Mandra glanced at them with a smile, then turned back to Scythe.

"Your only friend?" she asked. "What about Cryl?"

Scythe shrugged. "I owe the wizard much, of course. When I was a stripling of perhaps your age — fifteen?"

"Fourteen — and a half," Mandra said.

"Near enough," Scythe went on. "Cryl plucked me from poverty, found a teacher to give me a warrior's skills, developed my Talent when it showed itself — as he no doubt has developed yours. He even made me small

47

glass coverings to make my eyes look normal. But I don't think of him as a *friend*. I'm . . . in his service, doing his bidding against the Enemy. As I'm doing now, riding to the Wellwood."

Briefly he told her about the message in fiery letters, and she nodded thoughtfully. "Cryl mentioned that name — the Wellwood — when he sent me here."

"You seem very young," Scythe said bluntly, "to be sent on a mission. With Mephtik abroad, the risk could be great."

Mandra drew herself up. "I'm not afraid. Cryl always says I have more courage than is good for me — my family call it recklessness. And Cryl said that my Talent especially would be needed — *beyond* the Wellwood."

"Interesting," Scythe said quietly.

"But who is Archer?" Mandra asked. "And this boy who must be saved?"

Scythe shrugged. "Archer is another of Cryl's collection of Talents. As for the boy, the wizard told me nothing. No doubt we'll learn more when we find Archer."

He gathered up his cloak and staff, sheathed his weapons, and together they swung up into their saddles. Back on the road, they moved at an easy pace, while Mandra chattered brightly about her home and family and about her experiences with their mutual friend, the wizard called Cryl. It turned out that her family believed she was on a prolonged visit to an aged aunt in a distant town, so her absence was explained. As she talked, Scythe seemed wholly at ease, enjoying her sparkling personality. But his unique vision was tirelessly scanning every detail of the landscape around them, especially as the late afternoon began to darken into twilight.

"Time to find a place to camp," he said at last. As ever, he did not need to turn to see her quick, nervous glance. "And now you've realized," he added, "that we'll be camping together at night as well as riding together by day."

She tossed her blonde curls. "That doesn't bother me in the *least*."

"Good," Scythe said with a smile, "because you'll be quite safe. Think of me as an uncle. . . ."

He stopped. Though not a breath of breeze was stirring in the deepening dusk, a small whirlwind had arisen in the middle of the road. It danced and spun before them, gathering dust and leaves and bits of twigs into its spiral. Then, as they watched, it swirled one final time and disappeared.

In the roadway, the debris that the wind had carried settled to the ground — into the clear shapes of letters, spelling out words.

MAKE HASTE
THE POISONER IS IN THE WELLWOOD
THE BLADE HAS BEEN USED

Silently they watched the debris lift briefly from the ground again, scattering the letters. Then Mandra turned anxiously to Scythe.

"What does it mean?" she asked. "What Blade?"

"I'll tell you as we go," Scythe said grimly. "And I hope your Pearl has strong legs. It's a long ride — and we won't be stopping on the way."

Chapter 6

Rescuers

Only about a day and a half later, eight people were sitting in the midst of a black and starless Wellwood night. Six of them were green-hooded soldiers of the Poisoner, clustered around a small fire, crossbows close at hand. To one side, Archer sat against a tree—still bound, but now with a length of heavy chain rather than the spider's web-cord. She seemed wholly recovered from the blow on the head. But her eyes were filled with anxiety as she gazed at Jarral.

Jarral was sitting near her, also chained, also unmoving. But he did not appear to be looking at anything. Blank-eyed and pale, he merely stared emptily into the night. But in fact he was seeing a great deal, within his memory, none of it pleasant.

Over and over he relived the moment when the icy tip of the Tainted Blade touched his skin. Over and over he saw again the horror that had awaited him when he woke from his faint — the red-smeared M on his chest, the leer of Prince Mephtik, the repeated promise of death in four weeks' time.

And the promise, also, of living with horror and anguish every moment of those weeks.

All this Jarral saw, endlessly repeated images in his tormented mind. He wanted to writhe, he wanted to scream—but he had learned that the soldiers struck him if he did either of those things. So he sat still, staring into the darkness, silent tears glinting on his cheeks.

The soldiers were growing slightly boisterous as a leathern flask went from hand to hand. Covered by the noise, Archer wriggled a foot or so nearer.

"Jarral!" Her murmur pierced the cloud of horror enveloping the boy. He turned his head, saw the concern on her face. "Jarral, things are not as bad as they seem. Someone will come for us. Just as I was sent to your aid, others will be sent to ours."

Jarral's face crumpled. "What does it *matter*? I'm going to *die* in four weeks!"

"No!" Archer's voice snapped with intensity. "There is one who can save you, Jarral. One who has great powers, who will know how to heal the Blade-wound. You must not despair!"

Jarral stared at her. "Are you just saying this to make me feel better?"

To his surprise, Archer grinned. "I am saying it because it is so, though certainly it makes *me* feel better." She glanced warily at the soldiers, dropping her voice. "The one who will help us is a wizard, Jarral. A man of great power, and great goodness. He has devoted his life to a struggle against the evil that overwhelms this world."

"You mean against Prince Mephtik?" Jarral asked.

Archer shook her head. "The Poisoner is only one of a number of lesser rulers in different parts of the world. They themselves are ruled by another — the world's evil Master, who claimed that mastery long ago. To us, he is the Enemy. The Unnamed Enemy — for to speak his true name can be fearsomely dangerous. He is a mighty sorcerer, perhaps the mightiest who ever lived, a high adept in the blackest of the Dark Arts. Those who know and fear him have their own names for him. Like Demon-Driver . . . Phantom Leader . . . Master of Fiends."

Jarral looked appalled. "I never knew any of this," he said faintly. "I'd hardly ever heard of the Poisoner before. And now all this magic, and monsters . . . and what . . . what was done to me. . . ."

"You must be strong, Jarral," Archer said quietly. "You have lived in a child's innocence, in the sheltering Wellwood. But now there is no more shelter. You must leave the forest just as you must leave innocence. You have shown strength already — for many in your position might have been driven mad. But now you must show more strength, and courage." Her voice softened. "Be sure you will not be alone."

There was a sob somewhere in Jarral's voice, but he fought it. "You . . . you said you were *sent* to help me. Why?"

Archer looked sombre. "The wizard whom I and the others serve sends me where he will, and does not always give his reasons. But I know that he keeps watch, when he can, on events throughout the world. Perhaps he *knew* that the Poisoner was ordered to destroy the village. Perhaps also he foresaw that you would be spared — and sent me to your aid, because I have known you."

"I still don't understand," Jarral said weakly, "*why* the village was destroyed."

"I am not certain," Archer replied, "but at times the Unnamed Enemy has ordered such horrors so as to destroy someone who might come to *oppose* him." She leaned closer, intently. "The wizard I speak of — we call him Cryl — strives to maintain a fighting force of . . . people like myself. Equally, the Enemy strives to find and destroy us."

Jarral was looking dazed. "Are these other people giants, too?"

Archer smiled. "No — they are like me only because they too have been born with very rare and special mental powers, which are called Talents."

Jarral remembered the Tainted Blade twisting like a living thing in the Poisoner's hand. "You mean magic?" he asked.

Archer shook her head firmly. "The True Magic is possessed by even more rare individuals — like Cryl — and operates in a different way. I will explain it another time. A Talent is an ability to make things happen by the power of the *mind* alone. Some can see visions of events far away, or in the future — as I can, sometimes, faintly. Some Talents can reach into a man's mind and make him do things, or see things that are not there. Some can send their own spirits, the 'astral self', travelling out of their bodies. Some can start fires, mentally. And some can move objects with mental power. That is *my* main Talent — so I can direct my arrows to their targets."

"The way you moved the Blade," Jarral said.

"Correct. But my Talent is not powerful enough to move heavy objects." She glanced at the rowdy soldiers. "I could unfasten our chains with my Talent. But it would not help me to face six armed men, barehanded." Her eyes grew fierce. "Or not until they grow drunk enough. . . ."

Jarral shivered. He had become so absorbed by all the new information that he had almost, for a moment, forgotten their plight. "Then you think this . . . Cryl . . . will send other people with Talents to help us?"

"Without doubt. He might even come himself, though that would be a great risk for him. The Enemy seeks tirelessly to find and destroy him. But Cryl's powers allow him to watch events — and sometimes foresee them

— anywhere in the world. He will know of our situation."

"Is Cryl as powerful as the . . . the Enemy?" Jarral asked nervously.

"Probably not," Archer said calmly. "But if he can gather enough Talents to aid him. . . ."

She broke off, startled by a sudden crashing in the woods beyond the firelight. The half-drunk soldiers whirled — and froze, eyes popping, as a horse burst into view. It was a glorious animal, raven-black and powerful, and it was ridden by a startling woman. She had long hair as black as the horse's mane, smooth pale skin, lips as scarlet as the skin-tight dress she wore.

As the soldiers leaped up, the horse shied and reared, flinging the beautiful rider from the saddle. Then the horse dashed away as she picked herself up, looking dazed but unhurt. Turning, she threw one horrified look at the six loutish soldiers, gave a muffled shriek and fled.

All six soldiers roared with cruel glee and charged into the darkness after her.

Jarral turned to Archer with astonishment, but the bow-woman looked just as bewildered. For long moments they listened to the soldiers bellowing and crashing through the lightless woods. Then they heard a different sound. Almost a gurgle, as if someone was choking or drowning. A moment later there was a strange gasping grunt — and then another. Next, a ragged howl was followed by an angry roar, more crashing in the brush, something oddly like a whimper — and silence.

After a further moment, Jarral heard unsteady footsteps approaching. A soldier staggered into the firelight, his sweaty face strangely calm, empty-eyed. Jarral felt cold shock as the soldier toppled forward like a felled tree, revealing the slim hilt of a throwing knife jutting from his back.

Looking again towards Archer, Jarral was amazed to see that she was grinning. Then the grin widened, and Jarral looked back to see a dark-clad, dark-haired man, fairly lean and not very tall, stroll into the firelight. He was holding a slim, curved sword, which he was wiping with a ragged piece of green cloth. He stooped, retrieved the throwing knife, wiped that blade on the dead man's tunic and slid it back into its collar-sheath. Only then did he look over at the two prisoners.

"Archer," he said calmly.

"Scythe!" Archer said happily. "I wondered if it would be you. Was that one of your girlfriends, on the horse?"

Scythe smiled thinly. "A girl, yes, and a friend, yes, but not what you think." He held out a hand, and Mandra stepped into the light, bright-eyed. "This is the Lady Mandragorina of Felley Hale, whose friends call her Mandra, and who can make people see whatever she chooses — such as raven-haired runaways on black horses, to tempt soldiers into traps." He made a mocking half-bow. "My lady, this is Archer, warrior and bow-woman of many Talents."

Mandra produced a cool nod. "Not so many that she can avoid being captured, it seems," she murmured.

Archer looked taken aback, then smiled wryly. "Forgive us for not rising, my *lady*," she said with cheerful sarcasm. A spasm of strain tightened her face — and her chains and Jarral's snapped apart and fell away. At the same time Archer's bow, arrows and hunting knife rose from where the soldiers had placed them and floated across to her waiting hand.

For a second Mandra in turn looked taken aback as the towering bow-woman climbed to her feet. But then Mandra tossed her head and turned her ironic gaze on to Jarral.

"And this will be the mysterious boy we were sent to save. Does he *always* let his mouth hang open in that unsightly way?"

Jarral had been staring dazedly, but at that he closed his mouth and glared.

"It is sad," Archer said easily, "that your ladyship's Talents do not include good manners."

That produced a similar glare from Mandra, and Scythe smiled again. "Nice to see you becoming friends," he remarked drily.

Archer laughed, then introduced Jarral, with a quick explanation of how he and she had come together. Shortly she had explained to Jarral as well the nature of Mandra's hypnotic Talent and also Scythe's Talent. And Jarral gazed astounded at the chill blackness of the warrior's eyes when the covering headband was removed.

But the talk began to make Scythe restless. "We should move — before Mephtik comes to join the party."

".He is elsewhere in the forest," Archer told him. "Seeking other survivors of the village."

Scythe nodded, but did not relax. "We had a message — that the Blade had been used."

"It has," Archer said tightly. "Open your shirt, Jarral."

Slowly, with the haunted look returning to his eyes, Jarral pulled the cloth aside. Scythe's face hardened, and Mandra paled, as they stared at the raw wound in the form of an M.

"Signed with the Tainted Blade," Scythe growled. "How long do we have?"

"Nearly four weeks," Archer told him. "Till the full moon."

Mandra looked at Jarral, all her sarcasm replaced by sympathy. "Does it hurt?"

He shook his head dully. "It's just cold and numb, like frostbite."

"Time enough," Scythe was saying. "We can get him to Cryl, or get him somewhere safe so Cryl can come to us."

Within a few moments they were ready to travel. Scythe had called Hob — who had his cloak and staff on the saddle — and Mandra had collected Pearl, while Archer gathered two of the soldiers' horses for herself and Jarral along with some food and containers of water from the soldier's packs.

As they mounted, Mandra was looking troubled. "I don't understand *why* we're doing this," she announced.

Archer looked shocked. "To save Jarral's life! Why else?"

"Of course," Mandra said hastily. "But Prince Mephtik must kill people all the *time* — and Cryl doesn't always send his Talents to help. Why has he done so *now*?"

Scythe frowned. "Must be that the lad's important. Which likely means a Talent. So he's probably the one Mephtik was aiming to kill, when he wiped out the village."

"It must be so," Archer agreed. "Perhaps the Demon-Driver had become aware of a Talent growing in the village, but had not singled out which individual. So he sent the Poisoner to kill them all."

Scythe nodded. "And Cryl also must have become aware of our young friend's growing Talent, and sent you to help."

"But I'm no Talent!" Jarral broke in, looking alarmed. "I haven't got any kind of . . . of *power*, or anything!"

"You wouldn't know," Scythe said. "Talents don't start to show until the age of twelve or so. Cryl can explain it all to you when we get to him — while he's fixing that wound."

Jarral might have felt heartened by that statement. But in that second his flesh seemed to turn to ridged ice, as he heard a sound — some distance away through the darkened forest — that was all too hideously familiar.

A pattering sound, with a faint breathy hiss. A sound that brought to Jarral's mind the nightmare image of eight long scuttling legs, and snapping venomous jaws.

Chapter 7

Wizard in Blue

"What is it?" Mandra asked, as Scythe and Archer halted, listening tensely.

"One of Mephtik's monsters," Archer said. "It helped him capture Jarral and myself."

"One of the Seven Widows," Scythe added.

"When I saw it, earlier today," Archer went on grimly, "I shot at it. But . . . I *missed* it."

Scythe nodded. "You would — even you. Those things can *sense* a missile coming at them. At the last second they leap aside."

Archer brightened. "Is it so? Then perhaps there is a way. . . ."

"But it means that the Poisoner is coming back!" Mandra interrupted anxiously.

"More likely the creature is ranging on its own," Scythe said. "Mephtik often lets them roam free, and it's fast enough to cover a huge area."

"Wonderful," Mandra said hollowly. "What other facts can you terrify us with?"

"Many," Scythe said, smiling. "The venom of the Widows will kill anything — their jaws are like shears — they can outrun any horse — they can climb anything. . . ."

"Enough," Archer broke in. "Let us ride." She glanced at the dying campfire. "I would pay a good price for a torch."

Scythe shook his head. "If it was just the Widow, I'd agree, for the monsters fear fire. But Mephtik may be near enough to see a torch in the forest. No, I'll lead, because I don't need light to see. Just let your horses follow Hob."

So they set off, tense and wary, through the blackness that was no different from daylight to Scythe. Hob moved at an easy trot, weaving in and out among the trees, with the other horses following single file. Jarral, still chilled by the distant sound of the monster, strained his ears for any repetition of the noise. But as none came he soon began to relax slightly into the steady rhythm of his horse's movement.

They travelled for more than an hour until Scythe called a halt. Leaving Archer with the two youngsters, he scouted on foot into the forest around them for any sign of pursuit. The others waited, their silence growing more tense, until at last Mandra broke it.

"Archer," she said softly, "surely the Widow monsters are *supernatural*. So your arrow wouldn't have hurt it anyway."

"The Widows are natural creatures that have been *enlarged* by magic," Archer replied quietly. "Not *created* by magic. They can be slain by human weapons."

"Those that hit their target," Mandra murmured sardonically.

"Archer never missed before!" Jarral burst out hotly. "Ever!"

"Keep your voices down," Scythe said from the darkness, making them all jump, "or Mephtik won't miss us, either."

"Did you see anything?" Archer asked him as he came back to them and swung up into his saddle.

"Nothing unusual," Scythe replied, sounding slightly edgy. "But the thing is out there somewhere. The whole forest has gone still as death."

"As it was after the village was destroyed," Archer said.

Jarral felt even more cold and shaky as the horses resumed their steady trot in Hob's wake. His back was crawling with the feeling that evil Widow-eyes were staring at him from the black depths of the foliage around them. . . .

Then all images were driven from his mind by a sudden breathy hiss — from above him. All the horses suddenly reared and plunged, whinnying with frantic terror. Jarral felt his feet lose the stirrups. Then he was screaming along with the horses as, with another penetrating hiss, a heavy body with eight widespread legs dropped and clung on to the neck of his mount.

The screaming horse fell sideways, flinging Jarral from its back. Vaguely Jarral heard a roar from Archer and Mandra's shrill cry amid the clatter of the other horses' hooves. But above all those sounds he could clearly hear the sickening crunch as the Widow's fanged jaws closed on the back of his horse's neck. The horse's screams were cut off as if a door had slammed.

The attack by then had taken no more than two or three seconds. But to Jarral, near hysteria, time seemed almost to stop, and every movement seemed slow and languid, distorted as if seen through water. From where he lay, only a few paces away, he saw in the darkness the dim shape of the monster lift itself slightly, saw the huge sack of its body swing round towards him. His imagination more than his vision saw the dripping fangs, saw the ghastly bulging eyes fix upon him.

He screamed again, a wordless cry, as horror swelled like a gale in his mind. He saw and felt the Widow's shiny legs twitch as if it was going to leap again. His scream soared up past shrillness into soundlessness as terror blanketed his senses — except for a final instant.

In that fragment of time he felt an odd warmth flash across his forehead. And a tiny tongue of flame leaped impossibly up from the ground, in the narrow area between where he lay and where the spider-monster crouched on the dead horse.

The light from the startling little flame glinted on the Widow's eyes as the creature seemed to hesitate and pull back. Then Jarral heard a deep musical note — and, as the Widow sprang away from the flame, a broad-feathered arrow and a heavy dirk suddenly struck together, deep into the bulbous body.

The creature seemed to contract, its legs pulling tightly in. It twitched and quivered, the jaws flexing. Then the movement faded, the eyes turning blank and empty as the Widow sagged into death.

"It did not dodge *that* shot," said Archer's voice, with satisfaction.

"No — we were too close," Scythe said, as the other three, dismounted, moved forward into the light of the little flame. "And it was focused on the fire."

"So Jarral *is* a Talent," Archer said softly.

The flame was beginning to flicker and die, but there was still light enough for Jarral to see the interest and approval on the faces of the others. He got slowly to his feet, blinking dazedly, trying not to look in the direction of the dead Widow.

"Seems he is," Scythe agreed. "Anything like this happen before, Jarral?"

He shook his head. "Never."

"His Talent's just starting to show," Mandra said positively. "He's barely old enough."

"That is so," Archer said. "And no doubt it showed itself now because he was terrified." She smiled at Jarral. "You would never have felt such fear in that quiet little village."

Jarral shivered, trying not to remember how he had felt facing the Widow, trying also not to feel frightened by the fact that he too seemed to have one of the eerie mental powers called Talents. At that moment he would have given anything to be able to return to the peaceful, ordinary way things had been before he had met Archer in the forest.

"It explains Cryl's interest in the lad," Scythe was saying, and the words dragged Jarral's dazed attention back to the overwhelming reality of what was happening. "A firebrand is quite a power. When he learns to control it, he'll be one of Cryl's most valuable weapons."

"Once Cryl has dealt with the wound from the Blade," Archer added.

And then they all jerked with a new shock. An unexpected voice had spoken from the darkness.

"In that you are mistaken," the voice said. "Cryl cannot deal with the wound."

Jarral could hardly take in this new astonishment. For him, too many terrors had gathered upon terrors in the past short while. His mind had retreated into a protective blank numbness. He merely stared, dumbly, at the slightly hazy human figure that floated in midair above their heads.

Vaguely, by what remained of the little flame, he registered the fact that the person was male, short and slightly plump, with pale hair carefully arranged to disguise its thinness. He was dressed entirely in different shades of blue, from the high-necked tunic and well-tailored trousers to the elegant shoes on his feet. His pale hands displayed several bright sapphire rings, and a larger sapphire shone from the clasp that held a short, sky-blue cape around his shoulders. His chubby face looked slightly smug and sardonic as he looked down at the others. But deep in his eyes, which were bluer than any sapphire, lay an expression that mingled intelligence, compassion and considerable strength of will.

"The riddling wizard himself," Scythe muttered sourly, as the hazy figure floated down to the ground.

"Cryltaur Tabbetang," the figure said warmly to Jarral. "A pleasure to meet you, young man, even in such distressing circumstances."

"He has a fire-Talent, Cryl," Archer said. "You *did* know?"

"Why else would I send you to seek him?" the man in blue said blandly. "Why indeed would the Enemy send Mephtik to destroy the village, if not because he too sensed a new Talent about to emerge?" The wizard looked again at Jarral. "A powerful new Talent, to be sure. More so than we yet may know."

"We'll *never* know, if the Blade-wound kills him in four weeks," Mandra said pointedly. "What did you mean, you can't deal with it?"

Cryl frowned at her. "I am here in my *astral* being, as you should have noticed." He gestured at the haziness around his body. "I would have to be here in my real self, my physical body, to wield the True Magic against the

64

Blade. And even then . . ." His frown deepened. "The Blade was tainted by a mighty demonic magic. I might prove unable to overcome it."

"You can try," Scythe told him. "When we get Jarral to you."

Cryl looked despondent. "That is the difficulty," he said. "I have recently . . . moved my residence. The Enemy located my previous hiding place and nearly captured me. Where I now live is more than four weeks' journey from here, even if you were to ride without pause. And I dare not come to you in person. Beyond the magical screens of my dwelling, the Demon-Driver would certainly sense the presence of my actual self. His search for me grows ever more powerful, and determined."

His words jolted Jarral out of his numbness. "Then . . . you can't help me?" he whispered.

"I have not said *that*, my young friend," the wizard replied, with an encouraging smile. "But the fact is that I must remain safely hidden away for some while — perhaps until the Enemy is diverted to some other activity."

"Can you not use your magic?" Archer asked, her brow furrowed with a worried frown. "To bring us, or Jarral alone, to where you are?"

Cryl sighed. "If I cast a spell to do that, it would make the clearest possible path for the Enemy to follow. I am running a grave risk as it is, in my astral self — and that is a use of a Talent, not the True Magic." A deep sadness grew in his eyes as he gazed round at them all. "You may not realize it, but in the last year the Demon-Driver and all his forces have been hugely intensifying their efforts against me — and my dwindling band of Talents."

"Dwindling? What do you mean?" Scythe demanded.

"Deaths," Cryl said darkly. "Talent after Talent has been located by the Enemy's evil gaze, and now they are no more. Flint fell in the west, and Reader, and in the east Ellistree and Hand, and others in the south and north. . . ."

Archer and Scythe had visibly flinched as each name had been intoned. "How many left?" Scythe asked bleakly.

Cryl hesitated. "If you three had not saved Jarral, there would be . . . three."

"Just *us*?" Mandra asked shrilly.

Cryl's nod was slow and heavy.

Scythe's voice sounded remote and metallic. "Then our way is clear. If the Demon-Driver is making a final, all-out move against us, there's no more point in hiding. Flint and the others tried that. Let's strike a blow while we can."

"What blow?" Mandra asked tensely.

"Cryl knows," Scythe growled. "It's what he's been leading up to. Getting us to go after Mephtik and his filthy Blade."

There was a long, shocked pause before the wizard spoke again. "It is true. Jarral's wound would indeed be healed if the Blade could be destroyed — along with the one who wielded it." His voice darkened. "The future is veiled and shadowed for mortal eyes, so very hard to read. But there have been signs . . . in wind and flame and the shapes of bones. . . . A time of great portent is approaching — and the Enemy knows it too, which is the reason he has struck so fiercely against me and the Talents. And somehow the centre of the portent is linked with Mephtik, and the Tainted Blade."

"But we would need an *army* to get to Mephtik!" Mandra protested.

"A few can get farther by stealth," Scythe told her. "Especially if they muster some very useful Talents among them."

Jarral was gazing wide-eyed from one to another during all the talk. Finally he turned to Cryl. "You . . . you *will* be helping us, won't you?"

"When I can," Cryl said warmly. "But I doubt if this array of Talents will need much help from me, at least at the beginning."

"You must understand, Jarral," Archer added, "that Cryl can never run foolish risks. Other Talents will come along, after us. But if Cryl is taken, there might never be another wizard willing — and able — to take up the struggle. Then the Enemy would be victorious — forever."

As Jarral shivered at those words, Mandra turned to Scythe. "Do you think we have a chance?"

Scythe shrugged. "What does it matter? I never expected to reach old age anyway. We might creep away and try to hide — but then Jarral would die, and the Enemy would still find us sooner or later, if he's looking as hard as Cryl says. But if we fight — then with some luck we just might manage to kill Mephtik and heal Jarral's wound." His thin smile was wolfish. "And that would please me — because I hate the Poisoner, and I've begun to like the lad."

"So say we all," Archer said firmly, and Mandra sighed and nodded.

"Then you should know," Cryl said sombrely, "that Mephtik is even now leaving the Wellwood, on his way back to his capital city. You are unlikely to overtake him before he reaches the city. So, to accomplish your task, you will have to penetrate to the very heart of his Stronghold."

"At least," Scythe said lightly, "that's the last place the Enemy will look for us. . . ."

Part Two

Garden of Torment

Chapter 8

Fugitives

"Now it grows more difficult," Archer said heavily. "The Poisoner's search for us has begun."

The four of them, with the three horses — Jarral behind Scythe on Hob — had descended into a narrow dell thick with dry brush. By then they were a considerable distance west of the Wellwood. After crossing the bleakness of the Far Barrens they had entered a region known as the Blackgrass Moors — rugged upland country, broken and difficult, but colourful in its contrast of dark grass and bright, flowering shrubs. It was a slightly more populous area than the Barrens, with small scattered villages and the crude huts of shepherds.

Through the haziness of that late afternoon, Archer's incredible long-range vision had spotted a cluster of people in the distance — but not shepherds or farmers, for their green uniforms were unmistakeable. The soldiers were too far away for *their* eyes to see the four travellers, so the four had time to find a hiding place in the dell. There they had dismounted, to wait for dusk.

"So Mephtik knows what happened in the Wellwood," Mandra said with satisfaction. "Won't he be annoyed at the death of his pet!"

"Enough to stop at nothing to find us," Scythe said tersely. "We'll be dodging soldiers from now on. And we're only about halfway — with time passing."

Archer glanced quickly at Jarral. But the boy, standing

calmly beside Hob, had apparently not heard. "Can we have something to eat, now we've stopped?" he asked hopefully.

Archer relaxed, while Mandra allowed herself a small proud smile.

In the days following Cryl's astral visit and the beginning of their journey, Jarral had begun to sink deeper into the blank numbness that was close to despair. What Cryl had said, and the wizard's inability to heal him on the spot, seemed an end to hope. He withdrew into silence and misery, as Mephtik's threat became real. The iciness of his wound was a constant reminder that he had entered a time of lingering death. Despite the brave plans of the others, Jarral was seeing the end of his life drawing closer, every moment of every day. And the horror of it was tearing at the very roots of his sanity.

So, to protect him, Mandra had used her Talent. She had reached into Jarral's mind and had raised a barrier. It was only a small barrier, but it lay within the boy's memory, preventing him from recalling certain images. He could remember nearly everything that had happened since he had met Archer in the Wellwood. But he no longer remembered the existence of his wound, or what was to happen when the moon was full.

Freed from the terrible awareness of approaching death, he had become almost his usual self again — still capable of being greatly frightened by what might be happening, but no longer prey to that mind-crushing depth of hopelessness and despair.

So the others smiled at his very normal request for a meal. Certainly there was no shortage of food, for Archer's arrows kept them well supplied with game. "Let us eat, then," Archer said cheerfully, reaching for their sack of provisions.

But then she staggered, with a grunt of pain, her hands flying up to her face. For a second Jarral thought she had been struck by an unseen missile — until he heard the words that came jerkily from her mouth.

"Attack . . . in the night . . . fangs beneath the soldier's hood . . . be still . . . *be still!*"

Jarral and Mandra stared, appalled, as the giant woman swayed. Then Scythe was steadying her with a sinewy hand.

"Archer has a secondary Talent," he told them quietly. "She gets glimpses of future events. Mostly vague and half-formed — but I've never known them to be wrong."

"Yet they are confusing," Archer said. She was recovering quickly as the vision released its grip on her. "There are rarely enough details to know where or when the event will happen."

"Or *what*, it seems," Mandra said. "You talked about 'fangs beneath a soldier's hood' — what does *that* mean?"

"We'll find out in time," Scythe said calmly.

"I don't understand!" Jarral burst out. "How can you have Talents that don't work very well? How can *I* have a Talent if it doesn't work at *all*?"

"You have it," Scythe said. "No doubt there. You just need to learn to control it."

"Normally you would spend time with Cryl, who would help to draw out your Talent as he has so many others," Archer added.

"Using magic?" Jarral asked uneasily.

Mandra looked disdainful. "Don't be silly. Talents are natural powers, not supernatural. Cryl uses his own mental Talents — he has several — to bring others along."

"It doesn't make any sense," Jarral said sullenly. "Your wizard has all that magic, and now you say he has Talents too, but he's safe somewhere and *we're* the ones out here hiding from soldiers. . . ." He frowned, his face clouding.

"Let me explain — about Cryl and the Talents and what we call the True Magic," Archer said quickly.

Jarral's face cleared as his mind slid safely past the barrier in his memory.

"Cryl must remain in hiding," Archer went on, "because the Enemy — the Demon-Driver — is searching furiously for him. Cryl does not know if he alone could stand against the Demon-Driver. But he is *certain* that he could not withstand the Enemy together with all his creatures."

Jarral's brow creased. "What creatures?"

Mandra sniffed. "Don't village peasants know *anything* about the world?"

Archer raised a hand to silence her and to forestall Jarral's angry reply. "To understand, Jarral, you must see that it has to do with the difference between natural and supernatural." And she went on to explain.

Because humans are natural beings, she said, the Talents — the strange powers of a few special minds — are natural powers. So a person's Talent could be strong or weak, just like any other natural ability they might have. But the True Magic is *super*natural power.

"That power," Archer said, "is not found within natural beings like men and women. Supernatural power belongs to supernatural beings — spirits."

"You mean ghosts?" Jarral asked, his skin crawling.

Archer shook her head. "Not spirits of the dead. I speak of spirits that were never human, or natural, though some will take human form. But then they can take almost any

74

form, as they can do a great many 'magical' things. Some spirits are enormously powerful, some have only limited powers. But it is always supernatural power — the ability to *change reality*, which no Talent can do."

Jarral was looking pale. "I thought that was what magicians did."

"The sorcerer's power," Archer said, "is in his ability to *call* spirits and *control* them, with spells and charms and so on. A sorcerer *draws* supernatural power from the spirits, and also requires them to use their powers as he orders."

"And these spirits belong to the . . . Enemy?" Jarral asked.

"Many do. The dangerous, evil ones, the demons, who have always been enemies of mankind. The Demon-Driver gained that name by his ability to summon and control them."

"And Cryl?" Jarral asked nervously.

"A high-adept wizard like Cryl," Archer said, "has other spirits to call on. Some are not evil but are neutral, and there are many spirits of the purest *good* — demi-gods, seraphs and such powers."

Mandra frowned. "Cryl told me that the good spirits have turned away from this world and all its evils. He said they are more and more difficult to call."

"No doubt," Archer said. "But Cryl still has his faithful Urauld. That is Cryl's own *familiar* spirit," she added, when Jarral looked puzzled. "Urauld is a good spirit of great power, a staunch friend and ally to Cryl for many years. Through him above all, Cryl works his wonders with the True Magic."

Mandra was looking dubious. "They're still not terribly strong. I used to tell Cryl he should try to reach the Elementals."

"What are *they*?" Jarral asked despairingly.

"Nothing important," Archer reassured him. "They are like spirits, but not like them. They have no real shapes, no real minds or personalities. They are simply *natural forces* that exist within the most powerful events of nature. Lightning, gales, tidal waves, river currents, fire, earthquakes . . . all such things contain the spirit-forces that we call Elementals."

"Could Cryl reach them," Jarral asked, "like Mandra said?"

"Lady Mandra should know," Archer replied firmly, "that Elementals are of the *natural* world, not the supernatural. So a sorcerer could not summon an Elemental with a magic spell. It is said that there have been people, in past ages, who could call up Elementals. But that would be a *Talent*, a natural mental power, not supernatural sorcery. Anyway" — she grinned broadly — "calling Elementals would be dangerous, since they are usually destructive and always uncontrollable."

Jarral rubbed his eyes, feeling dazed and troubled. Understanding more about this frightening world — with its magic and demons and powers — was not at all comfortable. Not when they were in the midst of an unfriendly land, hiding from soldiers and perhaps from monsters.

Another frown creased his brow. It was so odd that he couldn't remember *why* they were there. He just seemed to have a hole in his memory. It worried him, much of the time, but he was not going to admit it to anyone. He had been growing almost at ease with his companions, despite Mandra's sharp tongue and Scythe's chill wryness. Yet he did not feel so at ease that he wished to seem a fool — or more of one than he sometimes felt.

"Jarral." Archer's voice broke into his unhappy thoughts, once more allowing his mind to slide past the barrier in his memory. "You must not think too many dark thoughts about the evil in this world. Cryl and Scythe and I are still alive, though the Demon-Driver and all his powers have been searching for us for years. We can continue to elude that search — I know we can. We must now merely gather our determination and courage and take one step at a time, one day at a time."

Scythe, who had wandered over to join them, smiled thinly. "And I doubt if old Cryltaur will leave us entirely on our own all the time."

"I hope you're right," Mandra said.

"I'm often right," Scythe said easily. "For instance, I'm right when I say it will rain tonight. So we can stay here and be wet and miserable — or we can seek shelter less than two hours' ride away, if no soldiers bar our path, in a comfortable inn famed for its food and drink and warmth of welcome."

"For *us*?" Mandra said sourly. "Would it be safe?"

"As safe as staying out here, with all the soldiers around," Scythe said. "Maybe safer — because the place is owned by a warm-hearted lady whom I know very well . . . and who is very fond of me."

And he turned towards Hob, as Archer chuckled and Mandra sniffed with disdain.

The inn-keeping lady, whose name was Charaya, was small and round and fair and energetic. She shrieked with joy at the sight of Scythe, calling him "Carver" and flinging her arms around him in an embrace that drew another chuckle from Archer and another sniff from Mandra. Scythe was again in his guise of a blind traveller, with eyes covered, and Charaya led him carefully to a table in the inn's ale-room, chattering merrily.

"I *knew* this was to be a lucky month," she bubbled, "and now you've returned to make it so, on top of all the extra business. . . ."

Scythe managed briefly to interrupt her to present his companions. Charaya was impressed by Archer, respectful to Mandra (who gazed coldly down her nose), and instantly motherly towards Jarral. In no time she and two maids had bustled about to produce a steaming meal and four mugs of fine ale. The ale-room was comfortable, there was no one else in the inn to threaten them with curiosity, and four clean beds awaited them upstairs. In his drowsy fullness after the meal, Jarral felt closer to contentment than he had felt for what seemed a very long time.

Naturally, it did not last.

Scythe, accepting another mug of ale, smiled at Charaya. "You spoke earlier of extra business, my sweet. Have you grown rich since I saw you last?"

She chuckled. "Would you stay, if I had?" But without waiting for a reply she went on. "It has been strange, indeed, though most welcome. Troop after troop of them, hither and yon on the roads, almost drinking me dry. . . ."

Scythe was no longer smiling. "*Who*, Charaya?"

"Soldiers, dear. Troops of them, in those ugly green uniforms. Searching for some fugitives, I gathered, from what they. . . ." Charaya suddenly became aware that her four guests were listening very tensely. Her hand flew to her mouth. "Is it you? Carver, are they searching for *you*?"

Scythe lounged back, and Jarral marvelled at how easily his smile returned. "Us?" he asked. "Charaya, my lovely, what would soldiers want with us? I am merely travelling in company with my friend Archer, who is serving as warrior-escort to the two young people on their way to the northern region."

Charaya relaxed, her bright smile returning. "I'm glad. Because it would have been terrible. Six soldiers passed earlier, and said they would come back for a drink after dark. . . ."

The words were barely spoken, renewed tension had barely gripped the four travellers, when they heard the sudden jingle of horses' harness outside the door, and the rumble of voices.

". . . And here they are now!" Charaya concluded brightly.

The door swung open, and six rain-wet, green-hooded figures clumped into the inn. For a fleeting fraction of a second the eyes of the sergeant in the lead began to widen with surprise. Then Jarral saw Mandra's eyes close, her face tighten, a frown gather on her brow. The sergeant relaxed, looking slowly around the room.

Mandra's lips moved, forming soundless words. "Don't much like the looks of this pig-pen."

"Don't much like the looks of this pig-pen," growled the sergeant.

"Let's move on, find a better place," Mandra mouthed.

"Let's move on, find a better place," said the sergeant.

The six men wheeled and clumped out again. A moment later thudding hooves signalled their departure from the inn.

"*Pig*-pen?" Charaya was flaring. "This place is as *clean*. . . ."

"Who knows how a soldier's mind works?" Scythe said soothingly.

"It was almost as if they didn't *see* . . ." Charaya began, then broke off with a glance at Scythe's covered eyes. "No, that's silly," she said briskly, and bustled off towards her kitchen.

"Well done," Scythe said quietly to Mandra, and Archer nodded admiringly. Mandra merely grinned, with a mischievous wink at Jarral.

But the occurrence, and general weariness, put an end to any dallying in the ale-room. Moments later, Charaya — looking upset because Scythe had gently refused her suggestion that they should have another drink, just the two of them — was showing her guests to their rooms. Jarral and Scythe were in a room near the stairwell, Archer and Mandra in the adjoining room. Each room was small but cosy, with two narrow beds.

"We sleep in our clothes," Scythe told the others when Charaya had left. "We might have to move swiftly, with soldiers around."

"Especially if any have fangs," Mandra said sourly, "as in Archer's vision."

But even that thought, on top of all the other fears that shadowed him, could not overcome Jarral's weariness. Yawning hugely as he settled himself on his bed, he toppled into sleep the instant his eyes closed.

It seemed only seconds later — though from the grey glimmer of first light at the window, it must have been hours — when some shapeless dream dragged him back to wakefulness with a jerk. The jolt shook his narrow bed, the mattress rustling and creaking loudly. He opened his eyes — and his body seemed to solidify into stone.

The creature rose, swaying, at the foot of the bed, obviously disturbed by Jarral's sudden movement. Its colour was not visible in the dim light, but the scaly, shiny, muscular length of it could be seen all too easily. A giant serpent, eyes glinting like fragments of metal, forked tongue flicking. And around the triangular head the flesh had expanded outward and upward, into a terrible threatening hood.

Jarral stared in paralyzed horror as the huge snake lifted itself higher from the bed, drawing its evil head back — poising itself to strike.

Chapter 9

Fateful Warning

As Jarral lay immobilized, staring at the serpent, a part of his mind became aware once again of a strange warmth building up across his forehead — the same sensation he had felt when facing the Widow monster in the Well-wood. But before the warmth could become stronger, the creature hissed and struck in a blur of speed, fangs gaping.

Until that blur met another, just as swift, as Scythe's curved sword flashed above Jarral's body and neatly severed the huge hooded head.

The serpent's body flailed aside, threshing in its death throes, blood reddening the bedclothes. Jarral flung himself from the bed, his stomach clenching, as Scythe sprang to the door. When he opened it, Jarral heard the faint sound of voices from the bottom of the stairs — and an odd metallic clinking, as if of coins.

"Sold us, by the gods!" Scythe snarled, turning. Jarral shrank back, for he had never seen such anger as showed in Scythe's face — a fury as black and cold as his sightless eyes.

"Come — quietly," Scythe hissed. Taking their few possessions, they crept out of the room and along the corridor, just as a number of booted feet began to climb heavily up the stairs. Noiselessly Scythe opened the door of the adjoining room, slid inside with Jarral at his heels — and halted. They were facing Archer with arrow nocked and great bow drawn, and Mandra behind her, dagger in hand.

At once the giant woman lowered the bow. "Soldiers?" she asked quietly.

Scythe nodded. "Mephtik's found us. With one of his hooded Najas, on Jarral's bed."

Archer blinked. "So — that was the vision, fangs beneath the hood. But how did he find us here?"

"We were betrayed," Scythe said shortly.

Then they all heard the footsteps in the corridor, the shout as the door of the other room was flung open.

"Archer, brace the door," Scythe snapped. "Mandra, Jarral, gather our things."

He sprang to the window, which was set low on the wall and looked wide enough even for Archer's shoulders. Flinging the window open, Scythe peered out and down, then swung round. By then the soldiers were pounding on the locked door, which would have quickly given way had it not been braced by Archer's broad back.

"All clear outside!" Scythe said, with a beckoning gesture.

Mandra and Jarral hurried towards the window as Archer released her pressure against the door and leaped across to join them, grinning.

Then her grin froze, and Scythe went rigid, and Mandra screamed.

Through the open window, death had burst into the room.

It came with a buzzing that was a roar. It came in a swarm of winged insects, shiny as if formed from bronze, each as large as Archer's thumb, swift and bright and entirely deadly.

Yellowjackets. The word formed in Jarral's mind as he stumbled back. The word meant nasty little insects with painful stings. But these yellowjackets were five times normal size, and there were at least three score of them, their poisoned stings glistening wetly like golden needles.

In the centre of the room, the yellowjackets swirled and circled. Then they seemed to gather themselves, almost as if they were being controlled, about to be hurled like a murderous weapon.

"Jump!" Scythe yelled. He half-pushed Mandra through the window, then leaped out after her. Archer turned towards Jarral, who stood rooted.

In that instant the soldiers battered down the door, and crashed into the room.

Once again Jarral was staring at inescapable death. In that flashing fraction of a second he knew that even if he jumped, the insects, or the soldiers, or both would follow. And not even Scythe and Archer could withstand that combined onslaught.

He did not feel Archer's hand on his arm. All he could feel, in that instant, was a totality of terror — until the other feeling arose once more. The warmth above his eyes, swelling rapidly into a raging heat.

And eye-searing yellow flame erupted from the floor, in a wall of fire directly in front of Jarral and Archer.

Dimly he heard the startled shouts of the soldiers. Dimly he heard the even more furious buzzing roar of the yellowjackets, as they swirled away from the fire that was the only thing they feared. Dimly, at last, he heard the screams as the maddened insects turned their fury onto the panic-stricken soldiers.

Then Archer simply plucked him from his feet, hurled him through the window, and dived after him.

They landed in a heap in the muddy stableyard. At once Archer sprang away, tugging Jarral after her. But he had an instant to glance back. No yellowjackets were storming out after them. Only yellow flames leaped from the window — flames that now filled the whole of the room they had left.

Then Scythe and Mandra appeared, mounted, leading two horses — which had belonged to soldiers. Archer half-flung Jarral into a saddle, and all four of them galloped at full speed across the empty moor.

Again Jarral looked back to see that the devouring flames had enveloped the whole of the inn. It was a beacon of fire, framed against the approaching sunrise, with ash and smoke rising in a tall grey tower. The four of them slowed, since there was clearly no pursuit.

"Your friend Charaya," Archer said to Scythe, "has lost her livelihood now."

"She deserves worse," Scythe said with a scowl.

"Why, *Carver* dear," Mandra said mockingly. "How can you speak so about your lady love?"

"She meant nothing to me," Scythe snapped.

"Just as well," Mandra said sweetly. "I wonder how much she was paid to betray us?"

"Forget the woman," Scythe said irritatedly. "What's more important is how it happened. How did the soldiers get word to the Poisoner so swiftly? And how did he get his creatures to us, just as swiftly? There's a smell of dark magic about it."

Archer frowned. "Mephtik is no sorcerer."

"His Unnamed Master is," Scythe said shortly.

"There is your answer, then," Mandra said. "But does it matter? We still must continue with the task. Unless you've changed your mind. . . ."

"No," Scythe snapped. His chill smile flickered. "Not when we have a secret weapon. Our young firebrand can make quite lethal blazes, can't he?"

"A valuable Talent, for us," Archer agreed. "There are none of Mephtik's creatures that do not fear fire."

"I still don't know if it *is* a Talent," Jarral said unhappily. "I can't make it happen when I want to. It only happens when I'm totally scared to death!"

"Lucky for us," Mandra murmured, "that *courage* isn't one of your strong points." Then she gazed airily away as the others frowned at her with reproach.

"No matter, lad," Scythe said. "You'll come to control it, in time."

"It may be," Archer said, "that even without Cryl we could help Jarral, along the way, to gain some control over his fire-Talent."

Scythe's thin smile reappeared. "If we can do that, we'll take Mephtik's city by storm!"

Then he nudged Hob, raising their pace to a mile-devouring canter towards the west.

Jarral was a little overcome by what had been said. But he was more pleased, rather than disturbed, to think that he probably did have a Talent, and an important one at that. As he rode along he tried very hard to make the strange warmth gather again, just above his eyes. But no matter how he concentrated, his brow remained frustratingly cool.

Archer noticed his frowns and strained grimaces, and after an hour or so she touched his arm gently. "Do not trouble yourself so, Jarral. We will work with you tonight when we make camp. Perhaps you can light our fire for us!"

As Jarral returned her smile, Scythe suddenly drew

Hob to a halt, with a muttered oath of surprise. Jarral tensed, looking round for some enemy, then tensed further as the sound from above drew his gaze upwards.

Swooping down towards them was a huge bird, like none that had ever existed in the world. It was long-legged and long-beaked, with a high crest on its head and an enormous wing-span. And its plumage was the brightest, most beautiful blue that had ever met Jarral's eyes.

"Have no fear," Archer murmured, as the bird settled on the ground beside them. "We have met this messenger before."

Jarral stared, puzzled. And then he nearly fell out of his saddle, as the bird opened its sharp beak — and spoke.

"I am Urauld," it said in an oddly musical voice, "as these others know."

Dazedly Jarral realized that the bird was speaking to him. Archer leaned over, still smiling. "Cryl's familiar," she told Jarral. "His spirit friend and ally, of whom I told you."

"Cryltaur has sent me," the bird went on, "because he dares not stir from his hiding place at this moment — not even in astral form. The Demon-Driver has become aware that you four may be the last living humans with Talents. So he has given Prince Mephtik further assistance to seek and destroy you. And he is pouring even more of his power into discovering Cryltaur's whereabouts. Our veils of secrecy are hard pressed to keep his searching magic at bay."

"Will they hold?" Scythe asked bluntly.

"We believe so," Urauld replied, "for we still have some strength in reserve. But it is you four, even with the boy's new-found Talent, who are in the gravest danger."

"Tell us," Archer said.

"The Unnamed Enemy," the bird said gravely, "has sent Mephtik a new aide and ally. He is one who, in this sphere, takes the name Flameroc. He is the reason why Mephtik was able to send his creatures against you so swiftly, once your location was known, this past night. Flameroc is terrible and powerful, and his power is supernatural. He is an evil spirit, from the first realm of the Farther Darkness."

Archer paled, and Scythe's face went as hard as carved metal. "A High Demon," he said bleakly.

"A most fearsome demon," Urauld agreed. "One of the primary beings from whom the Enemy draws his power. So the dangers facing you now are great. To save the boy, *and* yourselves, you must not only survive to confront and destroy the Poisoner. You must also face the monstrous evil of Flameroc."

Chapter 10

Demonic Talons

Archer stared at the bright blue bird. "I have never seen a demon," she said. "I had hoped to live all my life without doing so."

"You may," Scythe muttered. "Your first sight of Flameroc may be your last moment of life."

"Can't Cryl help us?" Mandra asked Urauld.

"He and I will seek to do so," Urauld said, "whenever we can elude the Enemy's search. But that grows ever more difficult and dangerous. For that reason I dare not linger here. Farewell — and good fortune."

The great wings spread, beating powerfully. With smooth grace Urauld swept upwards, growing hazy as he rose, until within a moment he had vanished utterly. Jarral stared upwards, hardly able to believe that he had met a supernatural being — and only half-aware of the others drawing slightly apart from him.

"What do you think?" Archer asked Scythe.

Before he could reply, Mandra interrupted. "What's there to think about? We have to go on."

Archer blinked. "That is great courage, for one so young."

"Not really." Mandra was pale and her voice was brittle, as if she could barely keep it from trembling. "I'm terrified — but nothing has changed. If Mephtik and the Enemy are hunting us, what does it matter *where* we go? So we might as well *try* to go on, as we intended."

"That's right," Scythe agreed. "Especially if Mephtik has a High Demon helping him. All we can do is keep going, as far as we can."

Archer glanced towards Jarral. "I say the same. The reasons for our task have not changed. But I do not see much hope for us."

"As you told Jarral," Scythe said, "take one day at a time. Who knows what might come along?"

"At least," Mandra added, "we might get some help from Cryl and Urauld, against a demon."

By then Jarral had rejoined them, feeling odd as always whenever anyone mentioned their 'task', since he never seemed able to remember just what it was. But he still felt reluctant to admit that to the others. Instead, he glanced once more at the sky and asked another question that had occurred to him.

"Archer," he asked, "if Urauld is a spirit, why does he look like a bird? Is he one of those *nature* spirits you told me about? Elementals?"

Scythe smiled mirthlessly. "Would that he was. We could use an Elemental, if we meet Flameroc."

As Jarral looked puzzled, Archer explained. "Urauld is no Elemental," she said. "He enjoys the form of a bird, but he is a true supernatural being, not a nature spirit. As I told you, Elementals are formless spirits without minds or personalities, who exist within the mighty forces of nature. Sorcerers cannot call them or control them. No one with that special Talent has existed for centuries."

"What does Scythe mean, then?" Jarral asked.

"Elementals are *natural* spirits, belonging to this world," Scythe said. "But demons don't belong to this world. They're supernatural and *un*natural, from the Farther Darkness. And there's something Archer didn't tell you before. Legend says that in this world a demon is always weakened, sometimes made powerless, just by being in the *presence* of an Elemental."

Jarral shivered mutely, chilled once again by the thought of strange nature spirits and evil beings from Farther Darkness. Then Mandra twitched irritably.

"If we *must* give lessons on the supernatural," she said acidly, "could we do so as we *ride*?"

For the rest of that day they rode steadily westward. As usual, the weather closed down over the Blackgrass Moors, with sombre, seething clouds whipped along by a slashing wind. The wind's hollow moan made Jarral feel even more uneasy as he stared around, half-expecting demons or Elementals to rise up from every bush or rock. The others were also keeping a careful eye on the countryside, to more useful effect. Many times Archer's eagle eyesight or Scythe's vision saved them from being discovered by patrols of soldiers. At other times, when the soldiers appeared too suddenly to be eluded, Mandra's Talent touched their minds so that they saw nothing. By twilight of that day, they had covered a considerable distance.

"Mephtik must have his whole army here on the moors, searching for us," Archer said quietly, as they made camp in a sheltered, tree-tangled gully.

Scythe nodded. "It'll get harder for us as we get closer."

"I don't understand," Jarral said, "why Mandra can't use her Talent all the time, so we could just ride past the soldiers?"

Mandra sniffed. "You don't understand *anything*. Using a Talent is very tiring. If I did what you say I'd be exhausted in no time. Especially when a bit of my Talent is working all the time to keep . . ." She caught herself just in time to keep from mentioning the barrier that she was maintaining in Jarral's memory.

"Also," Archer said, taking Jarral's attention away from what had almost been said, "we will need Mandra's Talent at full strength to disguise us when we reach Xicanti City."

Jarral nodded, feeling a little dazed as ever by all the strange new information. "At least we'll have the darkness to hide us now," he said.

Archer turned towards the west. The dark clouds looked as if they were streaming down a funnel towards the horizon where the sun had set, its last rays staining the clouds an ominous red. "Only from the *human* searchers," she said gloomily.

By then, as Archer turned to bring out some food, Scythe had vanished into the dusk for a careful scout around. When he returned, with an armful of firewood, their camp was ready. Meanwhile, Mandra had been using her Talent to probe Jarral's mind, to see if somehow she could help him to gain control over *his* Talent.

Jarral found the process disturbing. "Are you sure you can't read my thoughts?" he asked warily.

Mandra frowned at him. "I've *told* you. Other people's thoughts are all jumbled and cluttered — because most of the time we think in our own private inner codes. No one else can *read* them. Don't be so silly."

Jarral subsided sulkily as Mandra went on with her probe. But in a moment she sat back, looking frustrated. "I can't do anything," she announced. "He's just too *young*."

"I have a name, you know," Jarral said sourly.

"I'm not sure if it really *is* a Talent," Mandra went on,

impatience and tension running away with her. "Not if it only shows when he's frightened. Maybe he just has a Talent for *cowardice*."

And Jarral completely lost his temper.

Red-faced, almost spluttering with rage, he grabbed Mandra by the shoulders. Though he was no bigger, he was at that moment much stronger, for he shook her like an adult might shake a child.

"*Stop* it!" he raged. "I don't care who you are — stop it and leave me *alone*! I'm not a coward! And I'm sick of you treating me like a *fool*!"

As he yelled the last word, he flung her stumbling aside and whirled towards the others.

"I can't help it if I don't know much about the world!" he shouted. "Or if I can't make my Talent work! I don't even want to have one! I don't even know what I'm *doing* here! So why don't you all just *leave me alone*!"

As he roared those words in a final burst of fury, his brow felt suddenly afire, as if clamped by a band of hot metal. And the small heap of firewood that Scythe had brought burst into bright flame.

It was so startling that Jarral's fury vanished at once. Scythe sprang back, Archer goggled, Mandra yelped. Then she gave a small, shaky laugh.

"My," she said brightly, "*think* what we'll save in flint and steel."

"*Mandra*!" said Archer and Scythe together.

At once she looked contrite. "I'm sorry, Jarral," she said in a small voice. "Sometimes my mouth says things, even things I don't really mean, before I can stop it."

"It is the effect of strain and fear," Archer said with a smile. "I become gloomy, Scythe grows more cold and withdrawn, Mandra's tongue becomes sharper — and

Jarral sets things afire. Indeed, his Talent now seems to burst out when he is angered as well as afraid. We should not rouse his temper."

And they were all smiling — even Jarral, a little shamefacedly — as they relaxed and began their supper.

But no one was relaxed the following morning. In a misty, clammy dawn they had broken camp and moved cautiously to the wind-scoured brow of a low hill, to survey the land ahead. Jarral had been told that they were now approaching the Serried Valleys, a succession of broad, fertile lowlands with ranges of rugged hills rising between them. Beyond the Valleys, still several days' ride away, stood their goal, the city of Xicanti. But as the morning mists began to clear, they saw from their vantage point that more than hills and valleys lay in their way.

Westwards, as far as even Archer's eyes could see, the entire countryside was dotted with small groups of green riders. They seemed to be moving in an organized pattern, sweeping slowly across the landscape. No copse or thicket went unexamined by some eyes within that army of searchers.

"Can we ride around them?" Mandra asked.

"Maybe — but not to the north," Scythe said grimly. "That's no direction to approach the city from." As Jarral looked at him questioningly, he explained. "The Poisoner has a special . . . playground, on the north side of the city, full of more of his monsters. He sends prisoners into it sometimes, for amusement. And none of them has ever come out to tell about it. Mephtik calls it his Garden of Torment."

"Then what do you suggest?" Mandra asked.

Scythe shrugged. "If the soldiers get bored and lazy, later on, we might slip through — with the help of your Talent. . . ." He paused, turning to Archer. "What are you looking at?"

Archer had been staring up at the sky intently. "A strange large bird, very high," she said. "It looks like a vulture. But I have never known vultures in this region."

Squinting upwards, Jarral saw nothing. And Scythe merely shrugged again.

"No matter," he said. "It won't be Mephtik's. There aren't any poisonous birds — not even vultures."

Archer nodded and lowered her gaze again to the distant soldiers on the terrain ahead. Then she stiffened. "See there, Scythe," she hissed. "In front of those evergreens. Do you see?"

Scythe's face tightened. "I see them. So — Mephtik has released the Widows."

Jarral's spine crawled icily as he strained his eyes to see where Archer was pointing. Then he saw them, looking tiny at that distance yet still terrifying. Six hideous creatures, moving in short, scuttling dashes, the morning light glinting from the shiny black legs and bulbous bodies.

Archer reached for an arrow, unlimbering the great bow.

"Waste of an arrow," Scythe said idly.

She shook her head. "I have thought about it. At first, in the Wellwood, that Widow could evade my arrow because it was at long range. But later, Scythe, you and I could kill it because we were so *close*. It did not see our weapons in time to jump away."

Scythe nodded. "So?"

"So I will use my Talent," Archer said with a fierce smile, "in a different way."

She pulled the bow back, and released. The bowstring boomed as the arrow shot into the sky. For a moment Jarral lost sight of it, then caught it again, a tiny glint of reflected light beginning to curve back down towards the ground. Jarral also saw that the leading Widow had halted — aware in its own uncanny way of the speeding arrow.

But to Jarral's eyes it seemed that Archer was a long way off target. The arrow was surely going to fall some twenty paces away from any of the eight-legged horrors. And apparently the Widows realized that, for they were not poised to leap to safety. They had begun to move forward again, as the arrow plummeted harmlessly down.

But in the last second Archer's face twisted, neck muscles leaping taut. And the flash of light that was the hurtling arrow swung impossibly *sideways*.

Before the leading Widow could move, the arrow struck its bulging body and skewered it like an insect on a pin.

The creature's legs jerked wildly as it lurched to one side, antennae flailing feebly. Then it stopped, seeming to shrink, collapsing in upon itself, and went entirely still.

By then the other Widows were scuttling frantically in different directions, while a group of green riders spurred their mounts forward anxiously. And on their hilltop, Jarral and Mandra were cheering as Scythe nodded appreciatively.

"Clever," he said. "Deflect the arrow with your mind at the last instant, so the Widow hasn't time to jump. You might get more of them that way."

"The others are out of range now," Archer said, peering into the distance. "But they may. . . ."

She did not complete the sentence. Without warning, Scythe had flung his lean frame against her, yelling "Down!" as his shoulder struck her. The two of them tumbled in a heap, with Jarral and Mandra just beginning to look startled.

At that instant the air was torn apart by a raging, grating shriek. By reflex Jarral and Mandra also flung themselves down as, above them, vast black wings threshed thunderously, and huge black talons raked through the air where Archer's back had been.

Chapter 11

Change of Direction

"The vulture!" Archer yelled, snatching an arrow even as she and Scythe sprang to their feet. In the same moment one of Scythe's throwing knives appeared as if by magic in his left hand, and the curved sword was free from the staff.

The huge bird was wheeling in the sky for a new attack, shrieking its battle cry. Jarral stared up, horrified. It was evilly hunched, with a scraggy neck and dusty black feathers. Its wings were enormous, the talons and the hooked beak looked like black metal, lethally sharp, and the eyes blazed scarlet as it hurtled down at them.

Then it screamed again, as Archer's arrow struck deep into its black breast and Scythe's knife took it in the scrawny throat. But it was a scream of evil triumph — for the weapons had no effect. Instead, both arrow and knife seemed to droop, as if melting. A second later, they had vanished entirely, save for faint tendrils of smoke.

And Archer and Scythe flung themselves aside as the monster swooped, slashing at them with its iron claws.

Jarral was glazed with horror at what had happened to arrow and knife. Beside him, Mandra was chalk-white, shivering, while the vulture soared above them screeching its challenge.

"It's a *demon*!" Jarral heard Mandra whisper.

The word seemed to root Jarral to the ground. He saw that Scythe and Archer were grimly awaiting the next attack, bow and sword ready, though they knew the weapons were useless. Then Mandra was getting to her feet, instinctively drawing her dagger. Jarral knew that he was looking at three people intending to die fighting — against a supernatural horror that they could not harm.

The vulture-demon wheeled high, screeching, its eyes like hot coals. With some surprise, Jarral found himself stumbling to his feet as well. And he found that within the frozen terror that gripped him, there was a sharp edge of anger — at the sheer *unfairness* of a battle against a demon that could not be killed by human weapons.

As the vulture-demon began its dive, a high, clear call sounded from elsewhere in the sky. A flash of bright colour appeared, hurtling downwards like a spear — of the most beautiful blue.

"Urauld," Mandra whispered, almost in awe.

The vulture hesitated, then flapped away to gain more height as the blue bird-spirit flashed down. Urauld's long sharp beak was truly like a spearhead as it stabbed at a vast black wing. The vulture squawked and swung aside, well aware that it was not invulnerable to supernatural weapons, including the bird-spirit's beak.

Jarral almost stopped breathing as he stared up, watching the winged beings whirl into their aerial combat. Urauld was by far the more graceful of the two fliers, and looked quicker and more manoeuvrable. But the vulture was swift enough, and larger, with the claws that Urauld lacked. Jarral did not need to be told what a risk Urauld was running — both from the vulture and from exposing himself to the eye of the Unnamed Enemy.

So he held his breath and watched with growing alarm as the battle went on. Urauld swooped and swirled and stabbed, a fighting blur of glorious blue. But the vulture evaded each attack, and countered with frightful blows of beak and claws and thundering wings.

"Can't we *help* him?" Mandra gasped.

"There is no way," Archer growled. "Perhaps Cryl will come. . . ."

But even if the wizard had been intending to arrive, there was no time. As the two beings closed on one another again, it seemed that Urauld's beak would strike home. But the vulture somehow jerked back in midair, so that the spearing blow drove harmlessly beneath one of the huge dark wings.

At once, like a black-feathered club, that wing slammed ferociously against Urauld's head.

He staggered in the air, wings faltering. And with another ear-shredding screech, the vulture flung itself after him, claws reaching out.

Jarral threw up a hand as if he was trying to reach up to the battle. "*No!*" he screamed. "You *can't!*"

The cry seemed to mingle equal parts of horror and fury — and another band of heat clamped round his forehead.

The black feathers on the vulture-demon's breast exploded into flame.

The demon fell back as if it had run into a wall. Its screech altered from triumph to terror. And then it simply vanished, as if it had never been.

Urauld sailed wearily down to land heavily, his eyes fixed on Jarral. "So it is true, as Cryltaur guessed."

"What is?" Scythe asked intently.

But Urauld shook himself and looked quickly round. "There is no time. You must flee with all the swiftness you can muster, as far from here as you can. With the defeat of the vulture-demon, it is likely that Flameroc himself will come. I could not oppose *him*, alone."

Jarral looked astonished. "Then that thing wasn't Flameroc?"

"No," Archer said, "a minor, low-level demon. . . ."

"You must not delay!" the bird-spirit broke in desperately. "You must flee now! Ride — *ride!*"

And he flung himself into the air, wings beating, to vanish in his turn as suddenly as the vulture had.

"Where can we go?" Mandra asked tremulously as the four leaped towards the horses.

Scythe grimaced. "Only one way now — where maybe even Flameroc won't think to look for us. North. Towards the Garden of Torment."

They galloped at full speed, until even Hob and Pearl were foam-covered and gasping, while the other horses — especially the one carrying Archer — were staggering. At last they halted, seeking cover within a stand of trees and brush. Only then did they dare to look back.

With relief, they saw no signs of pursuit. Not even Archer's eyes could detect green uniforms — or worse — behind them. But all of them saw something strange and eerie in the distance.

The day had grown fairly clear and bright, and yet a darkness had fallen on one small area. It was as if something they could not see was blocking the daylight from that spot — which was the hilltop where they had faced the vulture.

"Flameroc is there," Archer said hollowly.

"Can you see . . . anything?" Mandra asked.

Archer shook her head. "The demon will be at the heart of the shadow he has brought, and I cannot see into it." A shudder shook her huge frame. "I think I am glad of it. I have seen one demon today, and wish to see no more."

Then she tensed, narrowing her eyes. "It looks — yes!"

she said excitedly. "The shadow is moving away — to the *south*!"

"The way we'd be expected to go," Scythe said. "So we have a breathing space. Let's use it."

For a while they walked, until the horses had recovered, then rode on at an easier pace. By midday they had still seen no signs of pursuit. But even so they were increasingly careful and alert, as they entered the populated farmlands of the Serried Valleys. Often they had to skirt stealthily around farms or villages, or seek cover to avoid other travellers on the dusty roads. But now only a few of those travellers were green-clad soldiers. And, best of all, they saw no further hint of that eerie shadow that had settled on the hilltop, and no menacing wings in the air above.

"It is odd," Archer said at last, as they stopped for a rest and food in another sheltering wood. "It would make sense to send a creature of the air to seek us. Do you think Jarral's fire *killed* the vulture-demon?"

Scythe shook his head. "Jarral's fire-Talent is *natural*. It couldn't kill anything supernatural."

Jarral thought of the arrow and the knife, melting to nothing after they struck the vulture, and could not help glancing nervously at the sky.

"But then *why* hasn't it come back?" Mandra put in.

Scythe shrugged. "Mephtik and his demon seem to be looking for us to the south. Flameroc probably has the vulture with him there. And I'd bet that Cryl, wherever he is, is doing something to keep Flameroc looking in the wrong place." His thin smile twitched. "But then I don't suppose Mephtik and the demon are feeling troubled. They'll feel sure that they'll have us in no time. After all, we're just four humans against two demons, the Widows and an army of soldiers."

"Four humans and Urauld," Jarral murmured.

"True," Scythe said. "And thanks to you, young firebrand, Urauld is still alive."

"You must be gaining some control of your Talent after all, Jarral," Mandra said encouragingly.

"No," Jarral said, looking glum. "I was just scared and angry, like always."

"Not like always," Scythe told him. "Before, you were just afraid. The anger is new. And, Jarral — anger is one of the surest ways of overcoming fear."

"As any warrior knows," Archer added. When Jarral looked surprised, the big bow-woman smiled. "Yes, even those for whom fighting is a way of life will feel fear before a battle."

"Courage isn't an absence of fear," Scythe said. "It's refusing to give in to fear — like you're beginning to do. So anger helps." His smile flickered. "Especially if it makes the enemy burst into flame."

The others laughed, and Jarral was still smiling a little when they regained their saddles and rode on. Perhaps he *was* getting braver, he thought to himself. It did not occur to him that courage had always been there, within him, waiting to be brought out. Perhaps its roots could be found within his fairly solitary life as a child in the Wellwood, which had given him a solid self-reliance that he could now draw on.

All the terrible things that had happened, all the attacks by ghastly creatures, had filled him with the most bone-freezing terror. Yet he remembered, in the vulture-demon's attack, he had been able to stand upright, to face with open eyes what he had believed would be the end.

He glanced around at the others. They had been very

kind, and approving, in what they had just said — about his courage. And the approval brought a strange feeling to him, something quite new, which at first he did not understand. But then he realized. Despite all the terrors surrounding them, Jarral had begun to bask in the warmth of being accepted, and liked — the warmth of *belonging*. The four of them were facing the dangers together as a unit, a group of *friends*.

Jarral had never had true friends before. And he suddenly understood that it was from their acceptance and approval, as well as from his own being, that he was drawing much of his new-found courage and inner strength.

But then a more uncomfortable thought struck him. There was the strange fact that he could never remember exactly *why* they were riding together, or where they were going. Before, he had tried not to think too much about that disturbing lapse of memory. But now, if he was going to learn to overcome his fears, he would have to face that one too.

He turned in his saddle, meeting Archer's kindly gaze. "What you said before," he began lamely, "about me maybe finding some courage . . ." He took a deep breath. "I'm . . . not so sure. Maybe I'm. . . . Maybe there's something wrong with me."

Haltingly he described the strange blank place in his memory, where his mind seemed to slip away, without remembering. Archer was frowning, looking troubled as if she was at a loss for words. But then Mandra, who had overheard, moved closer.

"Lots of people have . . . lapses," Mandra said, "when their mind goes blank about something. It'll probably all come back to you sometime, by itself. It *certainly* doesn't mean there's anything wrong with you. And I doubt if it has anything to do with how much braver you've been getting about things."

Jarral stared at her suspiciously. Yet there had not been the slightest tinge of sarcasm in her voice. "Do *you* think I have, too?" he asked.

"Yes, I do," Mandra said firmly. "And it makes me all the more sorry for calling you cowardly before. I hope you've forgiven me."

Jarral replied almost without thinking. "That's all right. I suppose you couldn't help being unkind, seeing how spoiled you are."

For a second Mandra drew herself up, mouth taut, eyes flashing. But then Archer spluttered with uncontrollable laughter, and even Scythe's smile almost widened into a grin. Mandra's lips trembled slightly — and then she burst into giggles.

Jarral laughed along with the others, not noticing the tinge of relief in their laughter at having again shifted the subject away from his memory lapse. In fact for some time all that Jarral noticed was Mandra — her melodic laugh, the curve of her lip, the brightness of her eyes. . . . It was as if he had never looked at her before, never seen how pretty she was. So he rode on almost peacefully, watching her when he could, no longer thinking very much about fear and courage, and blank places in his memory.

The following day or two proved uneventful, if tiring with the constant need for caution and battle-readiness. But there were far fewer villages and farms in the country around — almost as if they had re-entered the Blackgrass Moors.

"We're getting close to Xicanti," Scythe said. "And the Garden of Torment. Sensible people stay away from it."

Those words made Jarral stare fearfully at the landscape ahead. But the country remained perfectly ordinary as they rode on. For the rest of that day and most of the next, they wove their way up through another of the stretches of stony hills that separated the Serried Valleys. Finally, on one brush-covered hilltop, Scythe drew Hob up and gestured.

"There it is," he said.

Jarral saw only a dusty slope leading down towards a narrow, slow-moving river. Beyond the river the land looked bleak and unappealing — dry, rocky, with some patches of half-dead grass, thorny brush and thin, scabby trees. In dips and hollows here and there, scummy water pooled on the surface of thick mud and bog, where foul-looking mists hung low to the ground. The entire overcast sky seemed to droop low over that landscape, covering it with a shadowy haze.

"The Garden of Torment," Scythe said. "The land slopes down awhile, then up again till it reaches the north wall of Xicanti City."

"How do you know?" Mandra asked, surprised.

"I rode around the Garden once," Scythe said. "Just to have a look. The river runs around most of it, and the city wall blocks off the rest. To keep what's in it . . . in."

"And to keep us out, it seems," Archer muttered.

"There's a way across the river," Scythe said.

Jarral and Mandra stared, astonished. "You mean we're going *in*?" Mandra demanded, her voice rising.

Scythe shrugged. "Somewhere there's a High Demon looking for us. If we bypass the Garden and look for another way into the city, we might ride right into him. But he won't think to find us here. It's our safest way."

"*Safest*!" Mandra said scornfully.

"And quickest," Scythe added. "We don't have many days left before the moon is full."

"What's *in* this Garden, anyway?" Mandra asked quickly, diverting Jarral from his puzzlement at the mention of the full moon.

"Poison," Scythe said shortly. "Just about every kind of poisonous plant and animal. And some of Mephtik's special creations. But nothing with wings. Nothing that might fly over the wall and attack Mephtik's city."

"Oh, *that's* a comfort," Mandra said acidly.

Jarral was looking frightened as well as puzzled. "It doesn't make sense," he said. "Scythe, you told us no one ever came out of the Garden alive. . . ."

It was Archer who replied. "None of Mephtik's prisoners, Jarral. But we are going in fully armed, with Talents as well as weapons."

"But what *for*?" Jarral burst out. "Why do we want to get into the city? And what's the full moon got to do with it?"

Archer blinked uneasily and began to turn to the others for help.

And that was when Mandra screamed.

Chapter 12

Mephtik's Creatures

Jarral whirled, just in time to see a weird, shadowy shape, about the size of a horse but with rather more legs, scuttle out of sight behind a distant thicket.

"Was that . . . another Widow?" he asked fearfully.

Scythe shook his head. "Looked like one of the poisonous little dagger-tails you get in the northern deserts. But a bit oversized."

"At least it was going in the right direction," Mandra said shakily. "Away from us."

By then Jarral had forgotten about the questions he had been asking before Mandra's scream. And there was no time to recall them, for Scythe was leading them down the slope towards the river that was the boundary of the Garden. There, to Jarral's surprise, he said that they must abandon their mounts, for the Garden was no place for horses. And, he added, on foot the four of them might manage to escape the notice of some of the larger horrors in the Garden.

"Hob will look after Pearl and the other horses," Scythe assured Mandra. "He'll keep them out of sight, and he'll stay nearby waiting for me, as long as he thinks I'm alive. He always has."

So, with some reluctance, the others released their horses — and Hob, knowing his business, at once led the small herd away from the river, back to the brush-covered hills they had just crossed. Then the four travellers set out to cross the river, surprised when Scythe showed them a place where broad, smooth stepping-stones lay just below the surface.

"These stones were here before Mephtik made the place over into his Garden," Scythe told them. "And none of his creatures can cross this way. Most of them are dry-land beasts that don't like water. And the rest of them would stay away from this water."

Jarral could see why. The creatures in the river were numerous, hideous and undoubtedly lethal. Many fish and most of the plants bristled with evil spikes that were surely venomous. Dozens of bulging, jelly-like sacs floated through the stream, trailing silvery stinging tentacles. And many of them, along with some spiny fish and eel-like things with fangs, were rising near the surface, wriggling up on to the stepping stones to get at the humans.

But Scythe calmly flicked them back into the water with his staff, while striding from stone to stone, with the others following. At last they reached the other side, where Jarral stared around anxiously. If the river had been so crowded with horrors, he thought, how many would be creeping through the grass and brush ahead?

They set off in single file, with Scythe leading and Archer protectively bringing up the rear. Jarral watched with some envy as Mandra unsheathed her slim dagger, to have it ready. "I wish I had a weapon," he said wistfully.

Scythe smiled. "A firebrand always has a weapon," he said. "But you can carry this if it makes you feel better."

He drew the heavy dirk and handed it to Jarral. In the boy's hand it looked like a short sword, sturdy-bladed and sharp. Delighted, Jarral hefted it and half-swung it—

then looked quickly at Mandra, expecting a mocking remark. But she merely smiled, which delighted him even more.

Scythe had also drawn his sword, and with his other hand used the staff to prod at bushes and tufts of grass ahead of him. Within the first few minutes the staff had been struck by two buzzing, gaudily coloured snakes and bitten by a small hissing lizard — while Archer, using her bow like a club, had flattened two more lizards rushing at them.

"Couldn't Mandra use her Talent," Jarral asked desperately, at last, "to *hide* us somehow?"

"Too tiring," Scythe said briefly. "At her age, trying to reach all these creatures with her mind, she'd be drained and exhausted in minutes."

"And even then," Archer added, "she could not hide us from the *plants*."

A moment later another lizard charged them. It was the size of a small dog, with a scaly, bumpy hide and glaring yellow eyes. It came at them in a blur of stumpy legs, mouth agape to show needle-pointed fangs. But suddenly it halted, in the midst of a stretch of coarse brown grass and weeds. It was as if it was being held fast — eyes bulging, legs trembling, hissing cry rising into shrillness. Then it abruptly fell sideways and was still.

Scythe stepped forward warily, then froze. "Look at the grass," he said.

Only then did Jarral see what waited there. Some of the weeds grew along the ground, half-hidden in the grass. From those stems long thorns jutted up, hardly visible, a venomous trap for anything that walked that way.

"Good," Mandra said tensely. "Let all the things in the Garden kill each other off."

"There'll always be plenty left for us," Scythe said.

As they moved on, circling round the patch of grass, Jarral felt an icy hollowness growing in the pit of his stomach. He wanted to stare at the ground, to watch for more deadly thorns — but he also wanted to watch the shrubbery on the right, the branches of the trees on the left, the misty expanse of low bogland up ahead. He could feel the cold sweat of terror on his skin, a tightening of his muscles that made his knees feel watery and his teeth nearly start to chatter. With every step he felt more cold and sick and wretched, as the horror of the Garden wrapped round him like a shroud.

Then Mandra, just ahead, stumbled over a stone, muttered an almost inaudible but startlingly vulgar word, then glanced back at Jarral with a grimace. "I'm so frightened I can't walk properly," she said.

Jarral blinked, as Archer snorted from behind him. "You would be a fool if you were not," the bow-woman said.

For Jarral, it was like a sudden sunrise. He had not stopped to think that the Garden might terrify Scythe and Archer as well as Mandra. They always seemed so steady and controlled. But he remembered what they had told him before, about courage being not the absence of fear but the victory over fear. And he could see that they were fighting hard for that victory just then. He could see the sweat on Archer's forehead, the tension of her shoulders. He could see the muscles jumping in Scythe's jaw and his white-knuckled grip on the sword-hilt.

They are afraid, Jarral thought, but they aren't paralyzed by it. And in that moment when Jarral clearly saw that fear could be controlled, he began to learn to control his own.

Some of the coldness began to fade from his flesh, some of the tightness began to leave his muscles. The Garden of Torment had become no less terrifying — yet somewhere within Jarral's being was a sureness, small but solid, that the terror was *not* going to overwhelm his mind.

Oddly, in the next short while, nothing came along to threaten that new sureness. The Garden seemed to have gone quiet, as if all the vicious creatures had declared a truce. There was even a spot of unexpected beauty, when they circled a pool of stagnant, stinking water and found a smooth, winding pathway made of white sand, leading to a high-arched little bridge, decoratively carved, that reached across a ravine.

"That looks nice," Archer said warmly.

"It's probably supposed to," Scythe said. "We might not like where it leads."

Archer studied the bridge with her eagle vision and her face darkened. "No, we would not," she said, reaching for an arrow.

When she shot, the arrowhead struck deep into the wooden floor of the bridge, just before the highest part of the arch. Under the impact of the arrow a section of the bridge fell away, hinged like a trap door.

"And what would we have fallen into?" Mandra murmured.

They moved forward, avoiding the path, and peered over the edge of the ravine. Jarral felt sick as he looked down, for the ravine was clogged with snakes, writhing and coiling together. Many were huge hooded monsters like the one on Jarral's bed at the inn. But there were dozens of other sorts — bulky ones with diamond-shape patterns on their skins, elongated ones that were black or green or multi-coloured, small thin ones as decorative as jewellery, and many more.

And the acid taste of nausea rose in Jarral's throat as he saw, among the mass of tangled serpent bodies, the white glint of bone — from scattered human skeletons and grinning eyeless skulls.

Archer led the way across the bridge — the only way of crossing the ravine — stepping calmly along the narrow edge of the framework beside the gaping trap door, stooping dangerously down into the opening to reclaim her arrow. Scythe and Mandra crossed next, Mandra looking even paler but still determined. So Jarral clutched the dirk tightly, gulped back the nausea stinging in his throat and followed.

He was to swallow that acid sourness, and shiver in the icy clasp of fright, many times more in the hours that followed. Yet he fought to keep a grip on his new-found courage, trudging manfully in the steps of the others. Scythe was leading them on a winding path, seeking open ground, well away from thickets of brush or stands of trees or murky stretches of swamp with their ominous mists. Even so, there were dangers aplenty that came to attack them wherever their path led.

Fanged snakes and lizards of all sizes still infested the open, grassy stretches. More deadly thorns hid within the grass, along with weird swollen pods that popped open as they passed, to release foul yellowish vapours. Several times they just barely avoided one kind of hooded serpentine horror that spat its poison from many paces away. And when avoiding those dangers they often nearly walked into others — including hairy, fanged spiders the size of dinner-plates, or tall weeds covered in bristling, poisonous filaments.

Some of their escapes were by fractions of seconds and breadths of hairs — but they were escapes. The astonishing vision of Scythe or Archer seemed always to see danger before it struck, if sometimes only an instant before.

Or nearly always.

The exception came after another strange lull, when they had not been attacked for several minutes. Perhaps they had relaxed a fraction, so that in avoiding one tangle of brush they passed slightly too close to another.

The monstrosity burst from it with a sound like clattering sticks. It was as high as a horse, and bulkier, charging in a many-legged, skittering run. It was almost upon them before they could move — huge pincer claws reaching out, and above the body the tail arching high, with its curved sting like a claw, shiny with deadliness.

Chapter 13

Unequal Combat

It had come at them from behind, so that as Jarral and Mandra stumbled aside with choked screams, Archer was standing alone in its path. The big woman managed to jerk away from one giant claw, fending it off with her bow. But the monster was lethally quick. Its other claw swept across and slammed against the side of her head.

Archer took one stumbling step, then collapsed in a heap. The pincer claws reached down to clutch and crush.

But before Jarral could find breath to scream again, Scythe appeared as if rising from the ground in front of those claws. The curved sword flashed, and one claw jerked away, deeply gashed, dripping pale slime from the wound. The creature reared back, turned slightly with furious speed — and the terrible tail lashed down with its sting.

Scythe met and blocked it with his sword, gripped two-handed. For a wild moment the monster's tail flexed again and again, the steel-hard sting stabbing and stabbing. But Scythe's blade parried each deadly stroke, in a ghastly imitation of a fencing match.

The monster seemed to pause, glaring with its many wicked eyes. Then Jarral found the breath to cry out. A *second* many-legged horror plunged out from the thicket, tail raised high, and skittered around behind Scythe.

The warrior's black eyes glittered, though his face was as expressionless as smooth marble. Raising his sword, two-handed still, he waited.

The monster behind him moved first, flashing forward, snatching at Scythe with its claws. But Scythe had moved at the same instant, slipping aside, slashing twice with the sword. Its razor edge sliced a chunk out of the creature's hard-shelled head, swept on to chop away a front leg.

The grating, clattering noise rose higher as the furious creature half-spun and struck down with its sting. At the same time, the other creature joined the attack. Their stings stabbed down, again and again, twin blurs of deadliness, in the same pattern of attack as before. And for nearly the first time Jarral saw, fully, the towering skill and inhuman vision of Scythe the Slayer.

He seemed constantly to be perfectly balanced, poised between the two horrors. Yet he was in continuous flowing motion, almost too swift for an ordinary eye to follow. The sword became a dazzle of steely light, flickering back and forth. Each movement parried one of the deadly thrusts of a sting, yet Scythe's speed gave him time as well to try an attacking slash or thrust of his own.

For more than a minute, which seemed a lifetime to Jarral, the hideous combat continued. Scythe seemed tireless, his movements smooth and precise, his sword like an endless barrier of steel between him and the grisly stings. Then, somehow, he managed the seemingly impossible. For a fragment of a second, he increased the speed of his counter-attack. Before either sting could fall again, he sprang forward, directly between the pincer claws of one monster. It was the one from which he had chopped away a leg, which slowed its response. Before it could evade or strike, Scythe slashed at one of the great claws, and drove his sword for half its length into one of the monster's eyes.

Then he leaped lightly away as the monster staggered, tail slumping, legs collapsing under it like cracked sticks.

And that was the moment when the second monster turned and ran at Archer.

The bow-woman was still down, still stunned. The creature was only a few paces away, sting raised. Jarral saw Scythe start to leap in pursuit, but saw his foot slip on a patch of the other creature's slimy blood. As he half-fell, it was clear that he could not reach Archer in time. The monster was poised over her, arched tail quivering.

The shriek in Jarral's throat came out as a whimper. He raised a hand, hardly aware that it was the one still clutching Scythe's dirk. But in that moment of terror, no band of warmth grew across his brow. For once, the fear and fury in his mind had found another outlet.

Blindly, taking a quick stride forward, he thrust the dirk with all his strength up into the monster's bulging abdomen.

By good fortune the blade's point found a join between two segments of the hard shell-covering. Slime gouted over his hand — and then the dirk was wrenched from his grip. The monster whirled, and the dirk snapped in two under the shell's twisting pressure. Jarral stumbled and half-fell as the sting struck down at him.

Once again Scythe seemed to appear out of nowhere. A wild leap had carried him on to the back of the monster, and his sweeping sword intercepted the downward-slashing tail. The blade bit deep, stopping the sting less than an arm's-length from Jarral's face.

The monster sagged, slowing as both wounds took

effect. And Scythe leaped down and finished it off in two flashing thrusts of his sword.

As the creature's legs crumpled under it in death, Archer sat up slowly. "What happened?" she asked.

"Scythe had a fight with some oversized dagger-tails," Mandra said, trying to keep her voice light.

"Not just me," Scythe said. He turned towards Jarral, who was half-kneeling, still trembling slightly. "We don't just have another Talent. We have another warrior." He lifted Jarral effortlessly to his feet. "I've never seen anyone so scared," he went on. "But you overcame it. You found your courage, and did what had to be done."

Then Archer was putting a powerful arm around Jarral's shoulders, murmuring her gratitude, and Mandra's smile was warm with approval. So Jarral's trembling faded, and he was beginning to feel quite pleased with himself as they set off again. He even managed a smile when Scythe pretended to chide him for carelessly losing the dirk.

And he felt better still a few minutes later, for the ground had begun to slope upwards. Jarral did not need to be reminded that that meant they had now crossed more than half of the valley that contained the Garden. Within an hour, Scythe told them, they should come to the outer wall of the city.

That news gave Jarral a fresh burst of energy. And his feeling of well-being was helped by the fact that these stretches of the Garden, nearer the city, seemed to hold fewer creatures, while those that did appear were all normal-sized and easily dealt with.

Eventually they came to a spot where the upward slope grew steeper, leading up to the vertical rise of a low cliff-face, slightly higher than Jarral was tall.

"From the top of that cliff," Scythe announced, "we should be able to see the city wall."

As they started up the loose soil of the slope, Jarral was certainly not the only one striving to think about the coming joy of leaving the Garden — rather than the darker prospect of entering the city.

Archer and Scythe were carefully studying the slope ahead, alert as always. But suddenly Scythe halted, stiffening, his sword drooping in his hand.

"What?" Mandra said anxiously, staring up.

"Behind us," Scythe said thickly. "An enemy we can't fight."

The others turned — and went quite still, as if turned to stone.

The land behind them was alive with an army of insects.

They were in their thousands, moving steadily towards the slope. Many of those thousands were ants, shiny red and black. Many others were humped, hairy centipedes. There were strange worm-shapes and ugly beetle-shapes. And all of them had been enlarged, as the yellowjackets had been, so that each insect was as long and thick as the hilt of a knife.

Jarral felt frozen and heavy, as if cold lead had been poured into his veins. He had a sudden image of the insect army swarming over them, injecting their poisons with each savage bite. Yet he could not seem to lift his feet.

"We'll never get away from them!" Mandra cried raggedly.

"We can *try*!" Archer roared. "*Run!*"

Impelled by her voice and a powerful push, Jarral began stumbling up the slope. Beside him, Mandra was sobbing softly while she clawed her way upwards. Scythe and Archer were just behind, as Jarral saw when he turned a fearful head to look.

The deadly army, sweeping like a dark tide towards them, had nearly reached the slope. Jarral felt that he could see all their thousands of tiny, malevolent eyes staring hungrily up at him.

"*Climb*, Jarral!" Archer bellowed.

He scrambled frantically on. As he climbed, he struggled to find, somewhere in his mind, the trigger to his fire-making Talent. He knew it was their only hope against the swarming insects. But at that moment there was nothing — no gathering of heat within his brow. Just a wetness, where the sweat of fear and exertion met the tears that squeezed from his eyes.

He saw that Scythe and Archer had hurtled on ahead, leaping to the top of the low cliff. Scythe straightened, turning, as Archer reached down to help Mandra up, shouting at Jarral to hurry.

At which point Jarral slipped.

He sprawled face down in the crumbly dust, sliding back down the slope a foot or two. Instantly he leaped up, fresh panic flinging him onward — for a swift glance showed that the tide of insects was only two or three strides behind.

"Jarral, here!" Archer shouted.

She was leaning over the edge of the cliff, reaching down with one great hand. One step away, Jarral's foot slipped again, and he saw with horror that Archer was about to leap back down, risking everything to help him.

"No!" he shrieked, and hurled himself at the cliff, flinging a hand up towards Archer. As the giant woman's hand clamped around his wrist, he scrabbled and kicked at the cliff-side, trying to propel himself up. One foot landed firmly on a solid ledge — a flat, craggy rock jutting for half its length from the cliff-face. But as he drove his foot down against it, it broke away, dragged out of the soil by his weight. Just in time, Archer lifted him smoothly upwards.

Below, the swarming sea of insects had reached the base of the cliff. But they were met by a sound so totally unexpected that Jarral thought it was an illusion.

An explosive gush of sparkling water, bursting out of the spot on the cliff-face where the flat slab of stone had jutted.

A second later, the gush became a torrent. The four travellers, astonished and disbelieving, stumbled back from the edge of the cliff as the ground beneath them started to shudder. In the next second the whole cliff-face collapsed, and a wall of foaming water cascaded down the slope, surging out on to the land below — where not a single insect of any sort could be seen.

Scythe shook his head as if to clear it, Archer grinned a huge delighted grin, while Mandra and Jarral sagged a little, suddenly weak in the aftermath of panic. But none of them turned away from the amazing sight of the water still spreading out across the land as the torrent continued to boom out from the cliff.

"Perhaps it is an underground river," Archer said at last. "When the cliff was weakened, as Jarral climbed, it burst free."

"I've never been so glad to see water," Mandra said faintly.

Scythe smiled. "Mephtik will be annoyed. His Garden's going to be a lake."

Slowly they turned away, finding that the land sloped up still farther from the cliff-top. But when they trudged the short distance up to the crest, they halted again, standing in silence.

Beyond the crest was an expanse of flat land, covered with more dusty soil and brown grass, a few outcroppings of white rock and some clusters of spindly trees. But for once the four were not looking at the terrain.

On the other side of that flat stretch rose a wall. It seemed to be made of the same white stone as the outcrops, carved into gigantic blocks. It seemed to loom into the sky, menacing, impenetrable.

"The end of the Garden," Mandra breathed. "We've done it."

"All we have to do now is find an entrance in that wall," Scythe said sourly. "And get through without being seen."

Part Three

Glistening Tower

Chapter 14

The Streets of Xicanti

The massive wall loomed even more awesomely when they were standing beneath it. Jarral could not imagine how such mighty blocks of stone could have been lifted upon one another. Yet Scythe seemed to think that getting through the barrier would not be difficult. That part of the city wall was a protection against the monsters of the Garden, not against human raiders. There would certainly be a gate through which Mephtik would have come to gloat when he had flung some victim into the Garden.

They waited a while, until dusk, before crossing the stretch of open land — in case there were guards on the wall looking in that direction. It was an anxious time, waiting there in the Garden. Yet, oddly, they were left alone. Scythe remarked wryly that the outrush of the underground river, or whatever it was, had no doubt drowned many of Mephtik's creatures and discouraged all the rest.

When the shadows were long enough they crept across the open space. A few moments more, and Scythe had located the entrance that they needed. It was an impressive gateway, with tall metal doors that were ornately decorated. They were also securely fastened on the other side.

"Time for the Talents," Scythe said to Archer and Mandra. "Any signs of life on the other side?"

Mandra closed her eyes, and in the twilight Jarral could see a pulse beating in her temple. She was reaching out with her mental power, searching for other minds on the far side of the gate.

"No one there at all," she said finally, in a voice that sounded strangely weary.

"Probably just a patrol now and then," Scythe said. "Archer, can you do the lock?"

"Certainly," Archer said. Her face and neck went taut as she fixed her eyes piercingly on the doors. There was a soft grating sound, a muffled clank — and the doors swung apart.

"It was only a set of large, plain bolts," Archer said with satisfaction.

Scythe nodded. "When we go through," he said, "we have two choices. Kill anyone we meet, or let Mandra make them see . . . something else. I prefer the latter, because it doesn't leave unexplained bodies — we don't want Mephtik and his demon to suspect that we're here. But it puts a strain on you, Mandra. Can you do it?"

Mandra was half-leaning against the wall, her face in shadow. "I'll do it," she said, her voice still heavy with weariness.

Archer peered at her with concern. "Mandra? Are you not well?"

"Just . . . tired," Mandra murmured. She seemed to sag slightly, and Archer threw a supporting arm around her shoulders.

"It is the strain," Archer said. "All the terror in the Garden, and then her efforts here at the gate."

"And the *constant* effort she's making," Scythe said. "It's drained her. I keep forgetting that she's still very young."

Jarral was gazing worriedly at Mandra, who was still drooping, eyes half-closed, in Archer's clasp. "What constant effort?" he asked Scythe.

"Can't tell you right now, lad," Scythe said, as Archer looked slightly uneasy. "But I think we'll have to tell you before long."

Jarral was mystified, but then his attention was distracted as Mandra stirred and straightened.

"I'm all right, really," she said.

"You will be soon, anyway," Scythe said, "once we're through this gate. And you can relax — Archer and I will take care of any trouble. If we have some corpses we'll just bring them here, to the Garden. Jarral, you stay with Mandra, let her lean on you if she needs to."

Mandra seemed glad to agree, and shakily glad to lean on Jarral's shoulder. He put his arm around her slender waist to steady her, and for that moment felt powerful and reliable and as tall as Archer.

Then they went through the gateway like four silent shadows.

On the far side, dimly lit by a few small, scattered lanterns, lay a broad grassy stretch running alongside a roadway made of smooth paving stones. To Scythe's vision, which made light of darkness, no living creature of any sort was there to see them.

Undetected and all in one piece, they had arrived in the Poisoner's city.

"This is a wealthy part of Xicanti," Scythe said as they slipped quietly through the shadows on the long stretch of grass. Behind them they had left the doors to the Garden solidly closed and bolted again. "Around here it's big houses and ornamental gardens. Probably some patrols of soldiers, but I'll see them before they see us."

"I'll be able to help," Mandra said. She was still half-leaning on Jarral's arm, which was continuing to delight him.

"Not till you're rested," Scythe said firmly. Jarral saw that he was leading them into even denser shadows contained by a thicket of flowering shrubs. "And you won't be rested," Scythe went on as they halted, "till you let go of that barrier."

"I *can't*!" Mandra said, shocked.

"I think you have to," Scythe told her. "Your Talent is vital to us here in the city. You have to be at your strongest."

Archer nodded. "It is true, Mandra. And there may be less risk, now, if you let go. We have all seen how . . . things have changed."

"I suppose so," Mandra said doubtfully. She had drawn away to stand unsupported, and that disturbed Jarral almost as much as the mysterious conversation.

"What are you all *talking* about?" he demanded.

There was a moment's silence, and then Scythe laid a hand on his shoulder.

"Jarral," he said quietly, "we have to ask you to show a lot of courage, again — more than many grown men might be able to show. We have to do that for Mandra's sake and for all our sakes. And I think you can do it. You've grown up a great deal, as we saw in the Garden."

Archer and Mandra murmured agreement, which pleased Jarral despite the anxiety he was beginning to feel.

"Back there," Scythe went on, "you found strength and courage you didn't know you had. You didn't run or freeze or faint. When you were needed, you *attacked* that monster. And I believe you still have that courage. You will need it for what we must do."

Jarral swallowed nervously. "What . . . what is it?"

"Some time ago," Scythe said, "a terrible thing was done to you. It filled you with so much horror that we feared it would crush your mind. So Mandra used her Talent to set up a *barrier* in your mind, to stop you remembering that thing. That's the blank place in your memory that you've been worried about."

"What was done to me?" Jarral asked, his voice trembling.

"If I tell you while the barrier is still there," Scythe said, "you'll instantly forget my words. The barrier must be lifted. Then you'll remember — and it will be terrible. But keeping the barrier there is weakening Mandra. And without her, we have no chance at all in this city."

Jarral turned, peering through the darkness at Mandra, seeing the sympathy and concern on her face. *For Mandra . . . for all our sakes . . .* Scythe's words throbbed in his mind. All I have to do, he thought wretchedly, is be brave about something so horrible it might drive me mad.

With his gaze still fixed on Mandra, he shuddered. Then he clenched his jaw, and nodded once. "All right," he whispered.

Mandra's eyes softened as she returned his gaze. Then they closed, for the brief space of a heartbeat or two.

And raw, shrieking horror struck Jarral like an avalanche, driving him to his knees.

The memories surged back, storming through his mind, bringing shattering terror and desolation. He saw again the Poisoner's sadistic grin, saw the evil glitter of the Blade, felt its icy edge slice through his skin, heard again the promise of the lingering death to come when the moon was full. . . .

Only vaguely he heard Archer say, "Scythe!" in an urgent whisper, and Mandra say, "We can't *do* this!" in a voice full of tears and pity. Vaguely he heard Scythe reply, "Leave him. He will break or he will not. This must be done."

The words were like distant echoes through the cataclysm of horror and despair in Jarral's reeling mind. And then somehow he heard other words, which had been spoken by Scythe just before. *You found strength and courage you didn't know you had.*

The statement seemed to lodge in Jarral's mind, where the horror-storms still shrieked and crashed. And from it he felt a kind of stubbornness begin to rise, slowly growing and swelling. It seemed to be made partly from the inner strength he had found in the Garden of Torment, partly from a desperate wish to help Mandra and the others, but also from a wild *anger* — a child-like fury that he should have been so assaulted by the Poisoner.

The stubbornness burgeoned in his mind, like a silent shout of defiance. And the storms began to recede.

It was not that he had lost his awareness of his wound and the lingering death it carried. It was simply that his new inner strength refused to let him be crushed by that awareness. That strength pushed back the horror, holding it at mental arm's length, where it could not threaten or damage him.

Slowly he raised his head, opening blurred eyes to look at the others. It had been no more than a minute since the lifting of the barrier had felled him to his knees. Yet he felt as if he had been fighting a punishing battle for a year.

"When . . ." he began, then choked, his voice raw and hoarse. "When will the moon be full?"

"Two nights from now, Jarral," Archer said, her face creased with sympathy.

Jarral closed his eyes against a fresh wave of horror. Then, as his new inner strength fought back again, he opened them and looked up. The sky was dark, so it seemed that the moon was rising late. For no logical reason, that made him feel slightly better.

He stumbled to his feet. "Then we'd . . . better get going," he croaked.

Scythe smiled his wry smile and nodded approvingly. Archer grinned, patting his shoulder. And Mandra leaned forward — and gently kissed him.

Then they all turned and slipped away into the darkness.

Scythe led them warily through that wealthy section and from it into more run-down areas. For some time it was a fairly uneventful journey, since few people seemed to be on the streets of Xicanti at night. So Jarral paid only minimal attention to their route. Instead, with a strange calm that seemed to be part of the after-effects of his mental turmoil, he found himself once again thinking about horror. But not the horror of what had been done to him. Now he was thinking of the horrors that were to come.

He knew that the four of them had already done things that many would have thought impossible. But what was to come, he thought, must surely be beyond any possibility. Vividly he recalled Cryl saying that, to heal the wound from the Blade, they would have to destroy both the Blade and its wielder. But how could that be done when Mephtik was so well protected, and when he had a High Demon at his side?

Again, desolation and despair howled through the corridors of his mind. But now it was not solely because of the approach of his own ghastly death. Now he was thinking of what seemed to be the almost certain deaths of Scythe and Archer — and Mandra.

Involuntarily, his fingers reached up to his cheek, where she had kissed him. And as the strange calm regained control of his mind, he knew that he could not let them continue. It seemed to him the most obvious thing in the world. They were there in the city to try to save *him* from the Blade-wound. But if he were no longer *with* them. . . .

He reached the decision at once. He knew he would be terrorized to the depths of his being, yet he now knew with some sureness that the terror would not crush him. He knew what monstrousness would be waiting for him, yet he felt that he could face it. For Mandra's sake, and the others. Within himself he felt the strange calm enlarging and strengthening, as if his own mind was putting up a barrier against thoughts of what was to come. He imagined it was like the calm acceptance of a warrior who must fight when he knows he cannot win. And it was allied, in Jarral, to a gladness that he would no longer be taking his friends into destruction with him.

He glanced around. Deep in his thoughts, he had continued being only half-aware of the surroundings. Vaguely he remembered seeing one or two people along the way, but Mandra must have dealt with them. And now they were in a sprawling rat's warren of narrow, stinking streets and alleys, a paradise for beggars and thieves and low-lifes of all sorts. Scythe seemed to know it well — he called it the Middens, Jarral recalled — and was leading them on a tangled course into its depths.

Jarral's chance came in a particularly dark and cluttered alleyway, with several narrower passages opening off it on either side. There they came upon a handful of drunken men, hunched and ragged. Jarral knew that Mandra would be using her Talent to disguise the four of them. But clearly Scythe and Archer were carefully watching the ragged group.

In that moment, when not even Scythe was looking at him, Jarral simply stepped into one of the dark side passages and moved quickly away, alone.

Chapter 15

Eyes of the Demon

The others became aware of Jarral's absence within moments. But despite their frantic dash back through the foul alleyway, rushing into the narrow side passages, they found no sign of him. Even though the moon had risen, huge and silvery, aiding their search, they could not find him.

Finally, in a safely shadowy corner, Mandra wearily sent her mental power questing out like a telepathic bloodhound, seeking some trace of Jarral's mind. But after a moment or two she slumped against the crumbling wall.

"I can't *do* it," she wailed, her voice shaky with misery and fatigue. "I'm not strong enough. I can't reach very far, and there are too many other minds around. I can't hear Jarral *any*where!"

"What does he think he's doing?" Scythe snarled.

Archer sighed. "I imagine he has fled because he believes it will save us."

"Then he's a fool," Scythe said. "Does he think we'll just quietly go home, now he's gone?"

"Perhaps he does," Archer said quietly. "Perhaps at least he hopes that we will not continue . . . with the task."

Scythe snorted. "Then he's twice a fool. The task remains, whether he's here or not, and we can't waste time looking for him now. He'll either die two nights from now, wherever he is, or we'll succeed and he'll be saved, wherever he is."

He turned and stalked away. Archer and Mandra glanced up briefly at the brilliant face of the moon, only a fraction from being a perfect circle. Then they followed, into the murky depths of the Middens.

A great many stinking passages away, Jarral had found a hiding place for the night, after a nerve-racking time of skulking through the darkness. He had found a small space under some broken steps leading to a disused shed. There he curled up, unseen by anyone other than some small furry scavengers. By then Jarral was almost as troubled by hunger and thirst as by fright, and was feeling more totally miserable than he had ever felt. That misery deepened when the moon rose — for then the Blade-wound on his chest grew even colder, beginning to ache and throb.

But despite all that, his weariness dragged him down into a sort of fitful sleep, from which he awoke feeling even more miserable. A grey morning had gathered over the city, with a penetrating drizzle. Stiff and shivering, with thirst and hunger now actively painful, Jarral crawled from his hideout and stumbled away through the alleys.

Before long he could ease his thirst by squeezing water from his rain-soaked shirt. And while hunger and general wretchedness still plagued him, the ache of the Blade-wound had faded with the arrival of the day. Also, as he plodded aimlessly through the Middens, the fatalistic calm that had arisen in his mind earlier returned to help him again, to keep fear and misery at arm's length.

So he trudged on, all that day, lost in his own doleful thoughts, ignored by the other miserable inhabitants of those alleys. Finally, as the rain-sodden dusk began to gather, he found himself beside a warped and cracked wooden door, which had not only light but some amazing odours coming through the cracks.

Nervously peering in, he saw what looked like a tavern, crowded with unlovely and dangerous-looking men and women. The interior was lit by a roaring fire and a few hanging lanterns, which added the smell of woodsmoke and burning oil to the other odours — which, for Jarral, were dominated by the scent of cooking meat and tangy spices.

His mouth began to water like a starving dog's. As if of their own volition, his hands pushed open the door and his feet carried him inside.

No one seemed to look at him as he sidled along one wall, trying to make himself small. But as he drew near the source of the cooking smells, a figure blocked his path, and a sharp, whining voice said, "Boy? What d'ye want here, boy?"

The man facing Jarral was short, skinny and smiling an unpleasant gap-toothed grin. Perhaps his size often made him a victim among those lawless alleys. So he was not missing a chance to victimize someone smaller.

"Say up, boy, what d'ye want?" the whining voice demanded again. Nearby several other men were nudging each other with coarse grins. Jarral was to be baited, a moment's entertainment.

"Hungry," Jarral muttered.

The skinny man snickered. "An' can ye buy food, boy? Have ye money?"

Jarral stared at the floor. Of course his pockets were

entirely empty. He had entered the tavern because he had hoped . . . he wasn't sure *what* he had hoped. Numbly he shook his head, trying to back away. But the skinny man reached out and grasped his shirt, dragging him back.

"No money, hah?" he said with triumph. "Come thievin', have ye? Think ye can thieve from thieves, do ye?"

Jarral did not reply but merely pulled back, twisting away. The sudden movement jerked his shirt free from the scrawny hand of the man, who lurched, off-balance. One or two of the onlookers guffawed, and the skinny man reddened with rage. He swung his hand in a vicious backhand blow that sent Jarral reeling back. Colliding with a table, he felt metal under one hand, a blunt knife used for eating. Without thinking, he clutched it as he straightened to face his tormentor.

The skinny man blinked, then a needle-sharp stiletto leaped into his hand. "So the thief thinks he's a knife-fighter? I tell ye. . . ."

There came a resonant *bong*, like the note of a large bell. And the skinny man rolled his eyes up and fell straight forward on to his face.

Behind him stood a woman, clutching the iron skillet that had felled him. She was not tall, but she was immense. She had bare arms bigger than Jarral's thighs and an enormous bosom that jutted like a cliff, outdone only by the astounding girth of her hips. She also had large and beautiful hazel eyes, which were blazing with wrath.

"Knife-fight with *children*, will he, and in my place?" she roared. "And the rest of you smirking and giggling and *sitting* there! I've a mind to fling the lot of you out, bar my door against all your pig-filth and stupidity!"

All the people around, Jarral saw, were sitting hunched and half-cringing, like schoolchildren, as the woman's fiery glare swept the tables.

"Some of you pick up the Whiner," she went on commandingly, "and toss him in the gutter where he belongs. The rest of you drink up and mind your manners, or more of you will find a night's rest out there."

As two men hurried to scoop up Jarral's scrawny attacker, Jarral found the bright hazel eyes resting on him. "You, boy," she said, "come to the fire. You can eat now, and then I'll find you jobs to do till the price is paid. Fair?"

"Yes'm," Jarral said eagerly, dropping the dull knife.

An hour later, he had engulfed an amazing amount of spicy stew, and was up to his elbows in scummy water, rinsing out the well-used drinking vessels. But seeing that his eyes were drooping and his yawns were huge, the big woman took pity on him. Asserting that, for a boy, he had worked well enough, she showed him a straw pallet in a nearby corner that would be his bed.

"Sleep peaceful, lad," she said. "No one'll trouble you."

So Jarral curled up, with another vast yawn, feeling warm and full and oddly peaceful. He knew very well what lay ahead of him, for nightfall had brought the return, slightly stronger, of the burning ache within his Blade-wound. But his mind seemed determined to cling to its calm acceptance and to avoid all dire thoughts. With the horrors mostly kept at bay, sleep came over him like a wave.

He awoke with a start, seeing the room half-lit with the

chill grey light of dawn. Resonant snores told him that he was the only one awake in the place. He rose, stretching, shivering slightly — not with cold but with the thought that had entered his mind at the moment of waking.

This is the morning of the last day of my life.

Yet as he looked firmly at that fact, he did not feel as if he would collapse with panic and terror. As he tiptoed out of the tavern, to begin the day that would end with the rising of the full moon, he felt the fatalism again taking over his mind — like an anaesthetic, freezing his thoughts into a sort of calm numbness.

A light drizzle was falling as he moved away through the choked alleys. He was wandering randomly, indifferent to where he might be when night fell and the moon rose. And in that indifference he was not at all aware of the small hunched figure drifting quietly along behind him, always keeping him in sight.

As the morning drew on he found himself beyond the Middens, nearer the centre of the city, where the roadways were filled with people — well enough dressed, for the most part, and obviously on their way to their places of work. They seemed glum, cheerless and tense, and Jarral understood that cheerfulness would be rare in the city of the Poisoner.

Then a sudden clatter of hooves made him draw back, into a dark niche between two buildings. He saw the people on the street turn, saw them grow even more tense. Then they were moving quickly, and the street was suddenly empty.

Approaching, in the distance, Jarral saw a troop of mounted soldiers. Then, as they trotted closer, he saw something glitter — and realized with a sick clench of his insides why the street had emptied.

The soldiers were riding ahead of a vehicle, a large carriage of sorts. The whole upper part of it was made of a clear, transparent material resembling thick, pale-green glass, formed in sections like the facets of an immense emerald. Within the carriage Jarral could see two figures, one larger than the other. And icy fear clutched at his heart as he saw the long white hair, the dark beard, the narrow frame of the slighter one. Prince Mephtik himself.

The Poisoner's thin face was twisted in an angry scowl, and he seemed to be talking loudly with much hand-waving. It occurred to Jarral that Mephtik might have just been to see how part of his Garden of Torment had turned into a lake.

By then the carriage was opposite Jarral's hiding-place. And the other, larger figure, who had been sitting motionless, muffled in a vast hooded robe, flung up a hand. The Poisoner abruptly stopped talking as the coachman dragged the carriage to a halt.

Jarral's eyes fixed in horror upon that hand. And then upon the rest of the larger figure, as it flung back the robe, pushed open a door in the side of the carriage and stepped partway out.

Flameroc, said a small terrified voice in Jarral's mind.

The demon was in human form, but only to a degree, for everything about him was wholly inhuman. Upright, he was enormous, nearly twice as tall as Archer. Yet he was unnaturally, revoltingly thin — as narrow as a skeleton. His ribs showed clearly, as did the bones of shoulder and elbow, hip and knee. His long crooked fingers tapered to curved tips of bone-like claws. His face was a craggy skull-face, with a flattened nose, no visible ears and a wide lipless mouth in which glinted sharp saw-teeth like a shark's. What sparse flesh and skin he had were stretched tight over the bones, and were a dull, flat grey streaked with dark orange, as if he were made of rusting metal.

But all of that was nothing, compared to the eyes.

They were pools of molten yellow, like the heart of a fire. No feature showed in them, no pupil or iris — just the solid golden flare. But wordless things were spoken by those eyes. Terrors were promised beyond human imagination or endurance. Mighty hatred showed in them, and cruelty, and murder, and a power that could rend mountains. As Jarral stared at those eyes, dark twisted shapes of horror writhed in his mind, clawing at his sanity.

He knew that the eyes of the demon were looking for him.

Somehow Flameroc had sensed his presence as the carriage passed. Though Jarral shrank back into the niche, whimpering in the depths of panic, he could see the hot glare of those eyes sweeping towards him like rushing flame. The courage that he had found, the numbing calm, were swept away like cobwebs as an ultimate horror grasped him. He saw the demonic eyes probing his hiding place . . . he could feel their monstrous fire. . . .

Panic swelled within him as if to shatter his skull, and he opened his mouth and screamed.

At the exact same instant, a muffled roar sounded in the street, drowning his cry.

He was only vaguely aware of the sound, in the extremity of his terror. But he did not fail to notice the trembling of the ground beneath him. All around, he could see the buildings wavering slightly as the ground shook. Small dislodged fragments of stone and plaster fell clatteringly on to the street.

The horses of Mephtik's carriage squealed and reared with fright, the coachman battling to hold them. In the carriage, Mephtik was staring wildly around, shouting. And Flameroc seemed to have half-fallen back into the heaving vehicle. As he raised a long clawed hand again, the coachman allowed the horses to take the carriage away in a headlong gallop.

The last rumbling echoes of the earth-tremor died away at the same time as the noise of the horses' hooves. In the silence Jarral sat where he was, trying to quell his trembling. He had no idea what had happened, since he had never experienced an earthquake before of any strength. But it had got rid of the terrible Flameroc, which was all that mattered.

Calmer, he struggled to his feet, blankly noticing that the drizzle had given way to pale sunshine. Around him the people were emerging fearfully from the buildings, with flurries of nervous talk. Something strange and different had happened — and such things spelled nothing but trouble in the Poisoner's city.

As Jarral stepped out of the niche, he saw that there seemed to be a general movement of people away from him. As he looked at them, puzzled, he heard a rough voice behind him, and felt new fear ripple icily up his spine.

"Jus' lookit," the voice said. "Right where the Whiner said he'd be."

Slowly Jarral turned. Four green-uniformed soldiers with short javelins stood grinning at him.

"First time that rat-whelp ever told the truth," another grunted.

"You sure this's him?" a third asked idly.

"Sure," the first one said. "Lookit the clothes. He's no

142

citizen. Serg'nt says this's prob'ly one of the four we was searchin' round the country for, the other day."

"All by hisself now," the second one said.

Jarral half-turned, as if to seek some kind of help or escape. But all he saw, lounging nearby, was the skinny form of the Whiner, staring at him with a leering grin. And then one of the soldiers hefted his javelin meaningfully.

"Jus' stay still, boy," he growled. "Prince Mephtik wants y' — an' he's gonna get y'."

Chapter 16

Poisoner's Plaything

Soon afterwards, in another part of the city, the Lady Mandragorina was driving a crude and filthy cart pulled by a sway-backed horse. A few passers-by might have smiled at the sight of such a pretty girl driving a very decrepit vehicle. But at least Mandra looked the part to some extent, since — like the others — the journey had left her mostly unwashed and rumpled, her clothes tattered and soiled. And certainly she was a less startling driver for the cart than a blind man or a giantess.

Scythe and Archer were hidden in the cart, under a pile of hides. Scythe had stolen the cart — during the disturbance caused by the strange earth-tremor — as a way to cross the city while giving Mandra's Talent a rest, for the later time when it would be all-important.

On the driver's seat, Mandra was looking pale and strained, trying to attract no attention, twitching with nerves when anyone on the street idly looked her way. So she almost leaped into the air with shock when a groan sounded from the cart behind her.

"What *is* it?" she hissed wildly, twisting around. "Scythe . . . !"

"It's all right," Scythe said quietly from the cart. "One of Archer's visions."

Archer's groan was turning into recognizable words. "Jarral . . . soldiers and shadows . . . the stones that shine. . . ."

"What *is* it?" Mandra repeated fearfully.

It was Archer who replied, in a despondent voice, as her vision left her.

"I saw Jarral," she said, "a prisoner — in some huge building, that seemed to be shadowy and shiny at the same time."

"The Poisoner's Tower," Scythe said flatly.

Mandra gasped. "Mephtik will torture him!"

"Maybe," Scythe said. "But he'll keep him alive. Mephtik wouldn't miss a chance to watch Jarral die from the Blade-wound, when the moon rises. So there's time."

Mandra shivered. "Time for what?" she asked hollowly.

"Time to do what we're doing," Scythe growled from within the cart. "Time to go and knock on the door of Mephtik's Stronghold."

Standing by himself in the middle of a vast cold floor, Jarral was looking upwards, at the unbelievable structure soaring high above his head. It was the structure that contained Prince Mephtik's throne room — a gigantic Tower, the dominating centrepiece of the Stronghold. It was magnificent, overwhelming, a fantasy in metal and stone. Jarral could hardly believe that a single building could be so immense. The expanse of the polished marble floor looked as if it could contain his entire village, with room to spare. Upwards, where he was looking, the Tower's vault was lost in shadowed dimness, so that the building seemed to rise roofless into the sky. And the walls. . . .

They were curved, with no sharply angled corners, and were built of fairly small blocks of stone, perfectly fitted. The blocks were multi-coloured, mostly in shades of green and yellow, and were polished to a gleaming mirror-brightness. With the colour and the shine, it looked as if the walls had been smoothly covered with the glistening, scaly hide of some colossal serpent.

No natural light entered that throne room, only the light from decorative lanterns here and there on the walls, and braziers at various places on the floor. So, despite the glistening walls, there were great pools of shadow in many parts of the throne room. They were not enough, however, to hide the huge works of art—paintings and tapestries— hanging around the walls, depicting beings engaged in activities that were obviously to Mephtik's taste. That was another reason that Jarral was looking up, so that his eyes would not be drawn to those sickening images.

Then, too, there was the disturbing area near to where he stood. It was like a wide but fairly shallow pit set into the marble floor. Jarral had not looked into it — for he could hear a number of unsettling sounds from within it, as if it was full of living creatures. And he had heard plenty of sounds like that in the Garden of Torment.

He was aware that the soldiers who had brought him were standing somewhere behind him, near the tall, lustrous metal doors that opened into the throne room. The squad of soldiers had gone silent upon entering, over-awed and nervous. About two dozen other soldiers stood in the shadows around the walls, on guard, also wholly silent. The only sounds in the room came from the chilling movements in the pit—and the low rumble of two voices.

The voices came from a broad stone terrace, like a stage, some distance ahead of Jarral. Its smooth surface was above his eye level, reached by long steps of polished stone. The terrace was lit by many more of the decorative lanterns, and around it hung more of the revolting tapestries. At one side was an ornate table holding different vials and flasks — and Jarral did not need to wonder about the nature of the fluids within them.

Dominating the terrace was a huge dark throne of shiny wood and metal, carved with images of men and women who were contorted into what had to be the farthest reaches of agony. On that throne sat the Poisoner, narrow face intent, deep in conversation with the hideous, golden-eyed figure of Flameroc.

From the outset the voices had lifted the hairs on Jarral's neck and turned his insides to ice. But as the moments dragged on, and he was ignored, some of his courage — or the numb acceptance — returned to him. A part of his mind had been noting the passage of time, so he knew it was well past midday. In not too many hours night would fall over the Tower. His final night.

Mephtik will probably hurt me very badly, Jarral thought, tightening his leg muscles to stop them from trembling. But it can't last long. Only till moonrise.

So he breathed deeply and gathered what inner strengths he could. And then he lowered his gaze, from the high darkened vault of the Tower to the two figures on the terrace.

The Poisoner was wearing a loose robe of livid green, with strangely beautiful necklets and bracelets — which then moved, writhing and twisting, revealing themselves as small, lethally beautiful snakes. Next to the prince stood Flameroc, immense and ghastly. It was easier for Jarral to look at him now, for he was again swathed in the large hooded robe. Yet from within the hood those monstrous eyes glared, bright as molten gold.

The eyes swung to meet Jarral's gaze — and for a moment Jarral swayed, feeling that the layers of his mind were being stripped away under that blazing stare. But then the demon's eyes shifted away, so that Jarral could catch his balance, as the Poisoner spoke in his high, grating voice.

"Captain," he said curtly to some officer behind Jarral, "you say your sergeant and his men found the boy because of a creature called the Whiner. What is he?"

"Highness," came the captain's voice, raw with tension, "he is a common pickpocket from the Middens. We have him in a chamber nearby, for he believes he will be rewarded."

"Rewarded? A Middens thief?" Mephtik laughed chillingly. "He will receive his due. Keep him where he is." He waved a hand languidly to dismiss the captain, whose sigh of relief was not quite inaudible. Doors closed behind Jarral as the Poisoner's close-set eyes, and the demon's blazing ones, turned towards him.

"You seem an unimportant worm," Mephtik said sneeringly, "yet we are told you have been travelling with the three rebels who have dared to use Talents against my rule — and who now, it seems, lurk within my city."

Jarral said nothing. He was fighting an inner battle against a newly paralyzing horror. Did the Poisoner's words mean that his friends had not left the city? But they would be captured too . . . !

"He is terrified, or ignorant," Mephtik said, smiling cruelly. "Or both. Are you sure, Flameroc, that he is the one?"

"There can be no doubt of it." The demon's voice was the deepest sound Jarral had ever heard, but totally without warmth or mellowness. It was like the rumble of a landslide in some frozen cavern beneath a mountain that had never seen the light of day.

"Then I shall torment him," Mephtik said with evil enthusiasm, "till he tells me where the three are. And when we have *them*, our Master will more easily gather up the rebel sorcerer Tabbetang." He paused as a thought seemed to strike him. "Unless, friend demon, your powers can learn from the boy where the rebels are hiding?"

"I have told you before, *Prince*," the demon said contemptuously. "I cannot read the pallid clutter of a human mind. Nor would I wish to do so."

Mephtik glared, then switched the glare to Jarral. "Boy! Say at once where the three rebels are!"

Jarral scraped together a few crumbs of courage. "I don't know," he said, in a voice sounding more shrill and shaky than he wanted it to. "And I wouldn't say if I did!"

"Excellent!" Mephtik cried, clapping his hands. "Then I can play with you! Oh, I shall make you die *so* slowly. . . ."

"Princeling," Flameroc's ghastly rumble broke in, "you are a fool. Unlike you, I have never seen the boy before — yet, unlike you, I recognize him. You cannot kill him slowly, because you already have."

The molten eyes blazed brighter and Jarral felt an icy breeze, which seemed to congeal his blood as he glanced down. His shirt had vanished. And the M on his chest was pulsing horribly, as if with a life of its own.

"Oh. Him." Mephtik sat back sulkily. "The whelp from the Wellwood. I had forgotten." Then he brightened. "But the moon is full tonight! So I can still play with him awhile, and then we can be entertained at moonrise. A death from the Blade is always amusing."

"Before your playtime, little Prince," the demon said, "I would question him. I cannot read human minds, but I can hear a human lie. He spoke the truth when he said he does not know where his companions are. I would hear him speak the truth again."

The terrible eyes flared once more. Jarral felt himself seized by invisible hands, lifted from the floor. Fresh terror fell upon him so totally he could not even whimper, as he drifted through the air up to the terrace, suspended before the demon's awful gaze.

"Tell me," Flameroc rumbled, "what you know of the earth-tremor this morning in the city. You were there, somewhere, for I sensed the presence of the Blade-wound."

Sweating and shivering, Jarral found himself opening his mouth almost without willing it. "I know n-nothing," he stammered.

"Ah, the tremor," Mephtik said, grinning. "It quite upset you, did it not, demon? Made you all unsteady. . . ."

He stopped abruptly as the molten glare swung towards him. "I told you," the demon growled, "I was merely unbalanced when the horses nearly bolted." He turned back to Jarral floating before him. "But it is clear that the boy speaks the truth. As I expected. For a moment it seemed that the impossible had happened. . . . But of course it could not."

"Ask the worm about the water in my Garden," Mephtik said sourly. "It's too much — floods and earthquakes. . . ."

"It is of no importance," the demon said. "The boy knows nothing."

"Then why did the three rebels bother with him?" Mephtik said, frowning.

"Doubtless they had some notion of saving him from the Blade. Perhaps with the sorcerer's aid."

"Saving him?" Mephtik tittered. "No one can be saved

from that deadly bite." His hand dipped into his robe, snake-fast, and brought out the Tainted Blade. Laughing again, he brandished it before him, sweeping its green-stained edge towards Jarral. But the swing brought it just as close to the dark robe of Flameroc.

The demon jerked back so violently that the hood fell away — revealing the sudden tautness of the skeletal face and neck, flinching away from the Blade.

"Ho-ho!" the Poisoner crowed. "How the mighty demon shies from the little Blade!"

Flameroc's deep bass bellow of rage was like the roar of a thousand tigers. Mephtik paled and shrank away as the demon's eyes flared. "You will presume once too often, fool!" Flameroc thundered. "One day, despite our Master's order, I will pull you inside out and carve my name upon your very guts!"

"Yes, yes, indeed, Lord Flameroc," Mephtik babbled fearfully, "it was a harmless jest, I meant no disrespect, I assure you. . . ."

The demon's shark-teeth flashed in a ghastly grimace. As Mephtik cringed, Flameroc flicked a glance at Jarral, which sent him wafting back to the floor below the terrace. Released, he half-fell, dazed by what he had seen and heard.

"Play your foolish games, Princeling," the demon was rumbling. "I will be better employed spurring on your underlings as they scour the city for the rebels."

Still glaring, the demon gathered his robe around himself, and vanished in a sudden rush of frigid wind.

Mephtik straightened, recovering his arrogance, fixing his gaze on Jarral. "Now, boy," he snarled, "let us see what extents of anguish can be achieved, before moonrise."

Chapter 17

Into the Stronghold

The battered cart rattled over the paving stones of a street lined with well-kept buildings and shops. In the driver's seat, Mandra looked increasingly nervous, since more people were looking at her and the cart, quite out of place in that more superior area. But their glances were without suspicion — and there were no soldiers in sight, from whom suspicion might have come.

Farther along, following the directions that Scythe whispered from within the cart, Mandra turned the tired horse into an even more impressive avenue. And there, instinctively, she pulled up, staring — as Scythe and Archer pushed the screening hides slightly apart so they too could look.

They were looking at an uprearing bulk of stone that was the outer wall of Mephtik's Stronghold. At the far end of the broad avenue was a mighty gateway, its stone surround carved horribly to show men and women, mouths wide in silent screams, being attacked by the most ghastly of venomous creatures.

"Pictures from a torture chamber," Mandra said softly.

The others were silent, studying the great gateway, where a single, immense metal door stood within the ghastly surround. As they watched, the door opened with a deep creaking groan, and a detachment of soldiers marched out, to take up positions around the gateway.

Meanwhile the soldiers who had been in those positions had formed up and were marching back into the Stronghold. The huge door closed with a metallic crash.

"I was hoping to get here in time for the change of guards," Scythe said. "Mandra could have walked us in with them."

"Do we wait for the next one?" Mandra asked.

"No time," Scythe said. "It's mid-afternoon already. Mandra, you'll have to make us seem like ranking officers in a carriage — with a message for Mephtik."

Mandra nodded, and they rolled ahead along the avenue. The detachment of guards at the gateway numbered fourteen, all armed with crossbows, all coming to attention as the cart drew near.

In front of the huge metal door, the guard-captain saluted stiffly, looking at Scythe and Archer, who were now in plain sight on top of the pile of hides. Archer glanced at Mandra with a smile. She was obviously making them seem to be *very* high-ranking people.

"We bring news of the rebels," Scythe said. "Open the gate."

"At once, my lord," said the captain. He gestured, and another soldier sprang to a small opening in the wall that clearly communicated to others on the inside.

"His Highness is in the Tower," the captain volunteered, "enjoying some . . . recreation. He may be angry if he is disturbed."

As Archer glanced worriedly at Mandra, who was beginning to show some strain at maintaining the illusion in fourteen minds, Scythe leaned forward. "He may be even angrier," he snapped coldly, "if we are delayed in bringing him our news."

The captain paled and whirled on the soldier who had

spoken through the opening. "Why is the gate not opening for their lordships?" he roared.

The soldier jumped, shouted through the opening, and the vast door groaned again as it swung open. As the captain saluted nervously again, Mandra shook the reins, and the old cart clattered through the gate and into the Stronghold.

But Mandra was not guiding it. Her eyes were still squeezed shut, her face drawn with strain — for there was another detachment of guards on the inside, standing at attention, and another captain offering a salute.

Ahead lay another broad roadway, but with only a few buildings along it, interspersed with expanses of a beautifully tended park — soft rich grass with clusters of delicate shrubbery and graceful flowerbeds. Fortunately it was a winding roadway, so that in a few moments they were out of sight of the guards at the gate. Then Mandra could heave a huge sigh of relief, slumping wearily in the driver's seat.

But a moment later she was tensing again, aware through her remarkable Talent that other minds were to be found behind the windows of the buildings overlooking the roadway. Those buildings were offices, barracks, storerooms and so on, where anyone might idly glance out at the vehicle passing by.

"I'm going to have to rest a moment," Mandra said through gritted teeth. "There's so *many* of them."

Scythe nodded. "When it's safe, pull off the road into the bushes."

So, shortly, Mandra swung the horse and cart off the roadway, at a spot where no buildings interrupted the sweep of the lovely park. And there they discovered the ugliness within the loveliness — the smeared thorns among bright flowers, the grisly, oozing fruit and fungi on the shrubs, the evil statuary of torment and despair standing here and there on the grass.

Mandra shuddered at the sight, then flinched again as a break in the foliage ahead showed them, for the first time, their ultimate goal. From the heart of the Stronghold Mephtik's Tower soared up, its glistening multi-coloured stonework looking even more like oversized snakeskin in the late, golden beams of the afternoon sun.

"Let's leave the cart and make use of all this cover for a while," Scythe said. "Give Mandra a rest."

She smiled gratefully as they climbed down. For a moment they all glanced at the distant Tower again, as they prepared themselves for the last stage of their journey.

And then a harsh voice struck out at them. "You there! Stand where you are!"

Mandra and Archer whirled. Four soldiers had come into view past some bushes, to one side. They were clearly a squad that patrolled the Stronghold's grounds, and their crossbows were flashing up to take aim.

Mandra went tense again, her eyes squeezing shut, and the soldiers jerked with astonishment.

"Where'd they go?" one said, as they began to run forward.

"Musta ducked into the bushes," another said.

They went past in a rush, plunging noisily into a nearby thicket.

"If you made us invisible," Scythe said calmly to Mandra, "they'll keep looking for us."

Mandra looked distressed. "It happened so fast . . . I didn't think. . . ."

Archer glowered at Scythe. "It does not matter, Mandra. You have done wonderfully. . . ."

But she was interrupted by voices that proved it did matter. A great many voices, raised in questioning and angered shouts — which mingled with pounding feet and clanking weapons.

"I'm sorry," Mandra said faintly, her eyes squeezing shut again. "There must be forty of them . . . all joining the search. I . . . I don't think I can handle them all."

Scythe's black eyes glinted, as his sword leaped from the staff. "Then Archer and I will whittle their number down a little."

He poised himself, and Archer calmly nocked an arrow, as nearly forty armed soldiers burst into view through the shrubbery.

Archer's bow was fully drawn, Scythe was an instant from leaping to meet the charge, when Mandra's cry held them back.

"*Wait*! Look at their *eyes*!"

It was clear at once what she meant. The soldiers were thundering towards the three of them — but were not looking at them. They were looking beyond them, into the greenery.

As Archer and Scythe stepped aside, the entire troop charged past, flailing through some shrubbery, vanishing deeper into the park. Scythe turned to Mandra, eyebrows raised, but she shook her head. "That wasn't me," she said wonderingly.

Scythe's chill smile flashed. "Then I can guess. . . ."

"No doubt," said a bright voice. "It was, as you surmise, I."

The three of them looked up, amazed, at Cryltaur Tabbetang, dapper as ever, smiling down from where he was standing — looking slightly hazy at the edges — on the topmost leaf of a feathery bush.

"What are you doing here?" Scythe demanded.

"How brusque you are, my dear swordsman," Cryl said, floating lightly down to the grass before them. He was garbed again entirely in blue — this time a long frock coat and trousers in royal blue, a high-necked shirt in powder blue and a silky neckcloth in midnight blue.

"Are you in disguise, as unwashed beggars?" he asked, surveying the three distastefully. "It's *very* effective — especially the fragrance." He drew a large blue handkerchief from a sleeve and applied it to his nostrils.

"We haven't had much time for bathing," Mandra said sharply. "We've been trying to stay alive."

"My dear," Cryl said, waving his handkerchief, "you *smell* like you have been dead for weeks." His smile was cherubic. "And you have not done well, have you? With young Jarral in the hand of the Poisoner, and moonrise only hours away."

Mandra's eyes flashed. "But he *left*. . . ."

"Don't," Scythe said roughly. "Our wizard knows all that — he's just being annoying." As Cryl beamed, Scythe went on in the same harsh tone. "He's also being foolish, showing up here with Flameroc around."

Cryl's smile faded. "I am here *because* of Flameroc, to some extent," he said firmly. "I have every faith in your abilities — but it has begun to seem that you might be a little overmatched against a High Demon. So I have decided to come and save you." His smile appeared again. "I confess that the four of you, the last living Talents aside from myself, are rather . . . important to me."

"But you could be *taken*!" Archer said worriedly.

Scythe snorted. "You saw him up there, Archer. We're

talking to his astral being, like before. Urauld would be here too if this was Cryl in his true body. But even he isn't fool enough to come here like that."

Cryl bowed. "How gracefully phrased."

Archer was glancing up at the feathery top of the bush, then at the faint haziness around the wizard's body. "I should have known," she said sheepishly.

By then the sounds of the soldiers had completely died away behind them. So Cryl — floating serenely along, a few inches above the ground — led them back to the roadway.

"But what do you hope to *do*, Cryl?" Mandra asked tensely. "If you're not here in your real body, you can't use the True Magic."

"True," Cryl replied blandly. "But even in my astral form, I can use my Talents. And I have several of those, as you know."

As if to underline his words, a wild-eyed group of soldiers suddenly burst from some bushes and raced past the four of them, seeing nothing.

"The truth is," Cryl went on, "I am here partly because I became aware how exhausted you have become, Mandra my dear. You have done wonders for one so young — but now I shall provide. I shall get us into the Tower and reinforce all your efforts to do what must be done."

Scythe nodded. "I thought you might join us. Especially if we got hold of the Blade. But it's still risky for you even in astral form, isn't it, with the demon around?"

Cryl's blue eyes surveyed them, and his voice lost all of its usual mocking playfulness. "*Risky*?" he echoed. "I have perceived, in the elements and the ether, that we are approaching a crucial moment. A major crossroads in the life of this world. It is a moment when we dare not draw back and wait fearfully for another day. It is a time when we must run *every* risk, take every strength we have and hurl it into the struggle, in the desperate hope that it will be enough to tip the balance our way. For if it does — the gains will be immeasureable, the victory beyond the most hope-filled dreams. *That* is why I am here."

He paused, and the silence that descended seemed to resonate with the weight of his words.

Then his impish smile returned as he waved his handkerchief airily. "In any case," he said, "Flameroc is not presently with Mephtik in the Tower. He is pursuing the search for you three in the Middens, where Urauld and I have laid some false trails. On the other hand, young Jarral *is* with Mephtik. And since we know how *sportive* the Poisoner can be — and since the afternoon is rapidly waning — I suggest we make all haste."

Chapter 18

Journey's End

The afternoon was indeed hurrying towards evening. As they drew near the Tower, the beams of the setting sun now coloured its glistening surface with a lurid crimson. At the doorway — even larger, more imposing and more revoltingly decorated than the Stronghold's outer gate — its guards stood unseeing, under the touch of Cryl's powerful mind. The four intruders simply marched in, Cryl's slightly hazy form still floating just above the polished stone floor. Not a glance came their way from the soldiers and green-robed servants moving here and there in the great hall beyond the door.

"You make it seem so easy," Mandra whispered.

"As do you, my dear," Cryl replied. "I can merely sustain it longer, since I am older and stronger."

"Then keep sustaining it," Scythe growled, gesturing with his staff.

They had crossed the great entrance hall unseen and unharmed, and had traversed a corridor of bright stone that lay beyond it. At that corridor's end they faced the huge gleaming doors that led into the throne room, and the further platoon of soldiers planted there.

"A refreshing sleep, I feel, for these fellows," Cryl murmured. As he spoke, the entire platoon slid to the floor with a breathy sigh, and the lustrous doors swung open.

As they did so, the throne room beyond the doors filled with an almost inhuman shriek of purest agony.

Scythe flashed through the opening, sword glinting in his hand, with the others at his heels. Then they all stopped, held motionless by the horror of the scene.

They were staring at the shallow pit that lay near the centre of the throne room. In the midst of the pit a short pedestal had appeared — a solid pillar rising only a few feet from floor level, like a tree stump made of stone.

The stumpy pillar was *moving*, as if it were alive. It shook back and forth, rocked from side to side, tipped and jerked, swung and spun.

Below it, in the pit, rose the sounds of the horde of lethal creatures, hissing and buzzing and scrabbling as if in anticipation.

Because, on top of the pillar, clinging to the smooth stone, was a naked human figure. Though the figure was half in shadow, with its back to Cryl and the others, it was clearly small, thin and youthful. The ankles were shackled with dark iron bands, but the hands were free — clinging frantically as the pillar rocked and shook, threatening to fling its occupant into the pit and the waiting horrors.

As the four watched, in that frozen instant, the naked wretch on the pillar shrieked again. The pillar had jerked fiercely to the side, nearly dislodging the clutching hands. On the terrace, bolt upright on his throne, Mephtik sat hot-eyed and grinning, his hand on the small lever that controlled the movements of the pillar.

Once again the pillar jolted and rocked, and the victim's voice rose in a howl that spoke of terror approaching madness. A fleck of spittle appearing on Mephtik's lips as he hunched over the control, totally unaware of the four intruders.

"Cryl!" Archer said anguishedly. "*Stop* him!"

"I will," Cryl said, sounding tense and worried. "But it is difficult here, with the demon-essence so strong. Almost *too* strong, with Flameroc absent. . . ."

He stopped with a grunt of surprise. Without the slightest warning, Scythe's hand had flashed up to his one remaining throwing knife — and buried it in the green chest of a soldier who had leaped silently out of the shadows around the far walls. Then other soldiers surged out of the deepening shadows. As Scythe crouched and Archer reached for an arrow, Cryl gathered himself and raised a hand, his face darkening with tension. The soldiers crumpled to the floor.

But in that time, when Cryl was focused on the soldiers, the Poisoner — still too intent to notice anything else — finished his game.

Twisting the lever, he had abruptly brought the pillar shooting swiftly up to twice its former height, its screaming passenger barely holding on.

Then, with a burst of manic laughter, Mephtik lowered it just as swiftly — retracting the whole of the pillar back down into the floor of the pit.

For a tiny fraction of a second, the naked victim seemed to be poised in midair. The small body was contorted, every muscle standing out as if sculpted — but silent, gripped by a terror too monstrous for any final scream.

Then the figure fell with a flail of arms and legs, down into the fangs and stings of the waiting monsters.

And it was Mandra's shriek that echoed through the Tower. "*JAR-RAL!*"

On the high throne, licking his lips as he stared gloatingly down at what was happening in the pit, Mephtik jerked as if he had been stabbed. His mad gaze swung towards the intruders — and then he went rigidly still. Cryl, red-faced with fury, had raised a hand and wrapped his Talent around the Poisoner like steel bands.

"I'm so sorry," Cryl said, his voice trembling. "I was too slow. . . ."

"That wasn't Jarral," Scythe broke in, sounding slightly surprised. "He's just there — in the darkness by the foot of the terrace."

As the others spun to look, Cryl said firmly, "This place needs more light." At once the lanterns and braziers blazed up with unnaturally high and brilliant flame. In that brightness, they all saw Jarral.

He was kneeling on the floor, eyes open, seeming unharmed. But he was not moving, not even blinking — just staring straight ahead as if unseeing. And the livid letter M was steadily pulsing on his bare chest.

"He is in a semi-trance," Cryl muttered, sounding strained as if he were trying to move some heavy weight. "There is a demon-grip on him. Flameroc has left great power behind him in his absence. . . ."

Slowly Cryl gestured. Jarral rose from the floor, like a puppet supported by invisible strings. He did not move or blink as he floated towards the others. As Cryl lowered him, he sank again to his knees, still blank-eyed.

"Let's pick him up and get out," Scythe growled.

"We must take the Blade as well," Cryl said. "And there are things here that disturb and puzzle me." He looked up at the huge throne, where Mephtik still sat motionless and wild-eyed. "Come, Prince," Cryl called. "You may regain the power of speech for a moment, and tell us things."

The Poisoner's eyes bulged with shock and fury as his voice returned. "It's *you*, isn't it? The rebel sorcerer, Tabbetang? You *dare*, in my Tower. . . ."

Scythe spat. "Why don't we twist his neck and be off before the demon returns?"

"A moment more," Cryl said calmly. "Mephtik," he called, "who is the one in the pit?"

Mephtik grinned evilly. "A small thief, the Whiner," he said, "who betrayed the boy." His eyes grew brighter, his grin more mocking. "The boy who dies at moonrise, wizard! The boy who has brought you and your fools here! But you cannot save him now — nor save yourselves!"

"I can," Cryl said sternly. "Your demon has departed, Poisoner — and no other in *this* place can stand against me."

Then he paused, startled, as Mephtik flung back his head and began to laugh. The laughter became a shriek, crazed and shrill. It rose high into the blackness of the Tower's soaring vault. And there the shriek seemed to alter, taking on the shape of a word, or a name, in some ugly twisted tongue.

As it resounded, high in the inky shadows of the Tower's summit, something stirred. The four intruders heard a scrape like iron on stone, a rustle as if of heavy cloth.

Then the chamber was filled with a grinding screech, like metal trying to saw through metal. And red-eyed, black-winged monstrousness plummeted down out of the vault, dreadful talons outstretched.

Cryl cried out as if in pain. "The vulture-demon! It is *here! Urauld!*"

His shout was still striking upwards when, with a sound like splitting wood, the gleaming blue form of Urauld materialized in midair.

The bird-spirit appeared once again like a blue-winged spear, long bright beak lancing forward at the vulture-demon. The vulture screeched and swooped aside in a thunder of dusty-black wings. For a moment the two great winged creatures swirled around the vast chamber, manoeuvring for position.

And Scythe grasped Cryl's shoulder and shook him as though he was weightless. "Cryl, you *fool*! This is really you — making yourself *look* like an astral being!"

"Of course," Cryl said absently, peering up at the swooping combatants. "I could not invoke magic against the Blade unless I was here in person. But I expected the astral disguise to protect me from the Enemy's eye."

"But Flameroc . . ." Archer said.

"He would have gone on pursuing replicas of you three," Cryl said. "Urauld has been seeing to that — until now."

Then he fell silent, for above them the aerial combat had truly begun — again. The vulture had suddenly swept in, claws raking, only to find Urauld veering smoothly past those weapons and counter-attacking with spearing beak. Again and again the pattern was replayed, attack and counter-attack, in a blinding thresh and flurry of great wings. For moments that seemed endless, the weird duel filled the air of the throne room, appearing almost an even match. Then suddenly the four watchers gasped as a slashing vulture-claw chopped some sapphire-bright feathers from Urauld's wing. But the bird-spirit seemed unharmed, swooping and stabbing as before.

"Cryl, can't you help him?" Mandra asked anxiously.

Cryl shook his head. "I would need Urauld's power to use the True Magic against a demon, even a minor one. And Urauld is too preoccupied now."

Then he went silent, biting his lip as Mandra cried out. The vulture had swept in again, dodging Urauld's beak, then striking with its own in a wicked sideways slash.

More blue feathers floated down through the smoky air — but now they, and Urauld's breast, were stained with crimson.

The vulture's eyes shone no less blood-red as it screeched in triumph. It attacked ferociously, again and again, hurling its full strength into the onslaught. And though Urauld evaded each attack, diving and swerving away, the onlookers could see that the ooze of blood from his breast had become a gush. His broad wings were beginning to beat more weakly, as he whirled away from yet another series of frenzied attacks by the demon.

Then Urauld seemed to droop and sag in the air, as if his strength had failed. The vulture shrieked once more, surging forward in a crash of wings, iron talons stretching out.

But just before they reached Urauld, the blue bird-spirit swung sharply round, cried out something in a language unknown to man, and buried his rapier-beak for half its length in the vulture-demon's heart.

The two beings spiralled downwards together, failing wings beating feebly. Pinned by that terrible beak, the dying vulture used the last scraps of its strength to tear and slash at Urauld. Blue feathers and red blood rained down to the chamber floor. Then, just in time, Urauld weakly pulled his beak free, as the vulture's corpse crashed to the floor, its acid blood bubbling and hissing on the polished surface. And Urauld settled to the floor nearby, his own blood pooling around him.

As Cryl and the others ran to him, the bird-spirit raised his head slowly. "The demon has brought my death, Cryltaur," he said softly. "No wizardry can heal these wounds."

Cryl dropped to his knees, looking stricken. "Urauld — friend and companion — how shall I go on without you?"

"You must," Urauld said, his voice growing faint. "Yet the future is dark. There are terrors and battles to come, Cryltaur, more potent than any we have faced." His eyes, still fixed on Cryl, were beginning to film over. "One last thing, while I still live. I know you will not flee, for you rightly wish to save the boy. But use the True Magic with my aid — and raise shields around yourself and the others."

Cryl frowned. "Why —?"

"Do as I ask," Urauld said, now barely whispering, "and with haste!"

Cryl nodded, and swiftly made some complex gestures, murmuring quietly. An odd silvery sheen seemed to appear from nowhere, wrapping itself round Cryl and each of the others — including Jarral, who was still kneeling motionlessly where they had left him.

Urauld seemed to shrink, as if folding in upon himself. "Do not mourn my departure, Cryltaur," he whispered. "I am merely being released . . . from this sphere . . . sooner than we expected. . . ."

The voice faded and was gone. The eyes went blank as glass. And from the eyes of Cryl the wizard, usually so bright and merry, something looked out that was immensely old and grim and weary.

"I don't know whether to mourn you or envy you, beloved friend," Cryl said softly. And he reached out to touch the now lustreless blue plumage.

But his hand never made contact.

The body of Urauld vanished in an explosion of searing fire. And as Cryl and the others jerked back from the sudden shocking blast, the throne room seemed to tremble under the impact of an enormous, thunderous, deep-bass roar.

Flameroc loomed above them, next to the throne where the mad-eyed Poisoner sat. His robe was flung back to leave him wholly exposed in his fury, towering and skeletal, metallic shark-teeth bared as he roared again. And his monstrous molten eyes were fixed on Cryl, with tiny yellow flames leaping out from them, as from the blazing surfaces of twin volcanoes.

Chapter 19

Cataclysm

"Weakling of a wizard!" Flameroc bellowed. "Your absurd deception has failed, your familiar is destroyed, you are powerless and in my power! Admit your defeat!"

"My deception served well enough, demon," Cryl said. He was facing Flameroc unflinchingly, chin lifted in defiance, though his voice sounded small after the demonic thundering. "And I am hardly powerless, as you must see."

In response, the demon's fearsome eyes flared white-gold. With a crackling crash, a force that looked like fire and felt like bitter cold lanced down at Cryl. But it struck the faint silvery sheen that surrounded the wizard. Like water split by a boat's prow, the demon-fire slid off to either side of the shield, flickering and vanishing.

Flameroc bellowed again in swelling wrath. Again his eyes blazed and flared — again and again magical forces struck furiously down at the shields around Cryl and the others. Each time they were deflected and resisted.

"Are we just going to stand here?" Scythe snapped at Cryl, in between attacks. "Can't you do something?"

"Without Urauld," Cryl said bitterly, "I have no magic to face a High Demon. But I still have my Talents, as all of you have yours. I merely need . . . the right moment."

As if in reply, something like a gigantic invisible battering ram struck at their shields. Cryl seemed to sway a little, but the shields held. From the terrace Flameroc's roar of fury seemed to shake the stone slabs of the floor.

Scythe's face tightened. "The shields won't stand much more of that. And what can mere Talents do against Flameroc?"

"One thing," Cryl said quietly. "They can awaken Jarral."

"Oh . . . Jarral!" Mandra said, realizing they had almost forgotten about him. Turning, they saw that he was unharmed, and no longer kneeling in that frozen, staring trance. Now he was lying quietly on his side, eyes closed. But the M on his chest was pulsing more furiously, as if a living thing fought to break through the skin.

"Before Urauld died," Cryl said, "I managed to break the holding spell that had been on him. He is now merely in a light sleep of my devising — and he too is shielded."

That was instantly verified. From Flameroc's volcanic eyes a stream of small missiles flowed, fragments of blistering fire like a burst of hot golden bullets. They struck against the silvery shields, rattling like a host of drums. Again the shields withstood the attack — but Cryl reeled, almost losing his balance.

"The shields are beginning to falter," he gasped. "It must be done — I can delay no longer."

"*What* must be done?" Scythe demanded.

"I must awaken Jarral's Talent to its full adult power," Cryl said grimly.

Archer looked puzzled. "A mere firebrand, against this enemy?"

Cryl shook his head, then took a deep breath as if

gathering himself. As he did so, from the terrace they heard Mephtik cry out. "Flameroc! I pray you, spare some of them for me! One, at least, for me to play with!"

The demon turned on him, snarling. "Silence, fool, or I will feed you to your own creatures!"

In that moment of relief from the onslaught, Cryl had turned urgently to the other three. "What I am about to do," he told them, "is our only hope. It may kill all of us, including Jarral. Because I must reach his mind with mine — and I cannot reach him through the shields."

"You want to drop the *shields*?" Mandra gasped.

"They are all connected," Cryl said. "If I abandon mine, all will go."

"They're going anyway," Scythe snapped. "Do what you can, Cryl. But do it *now*!"

The others looked up. Flameroc seemed to have grown even more elongated, as he raised his skeletal arms above his head, fingers like bony claws. Some of the cold fire flickered around those claws, danced around the huge body like an aura. And the terrible eyes altered once again.

Their molten gold swelled and brightened into a colourless white heat. And in turn, the whiteness intensified. From the painful white of a polar sun on new snow, it grew brighter. From the blinding white of raw magnesium erupting into flame, it grew brighter. Mandra and Archer and even Cryl flung hands over their faces, so that Scythe stood alone, his black eyes shiny with reflections of the demon's white fire, facing Flameroc with a defiant snarl.

The monstrous eyes swelled further, their whiteness now like that of a star blooming into the final convulsion of a nova. As that irresistible radiance focused, Cryl turned his back on it to face Jarral.

"Jarral!" As he spoke, his voice clear as a bell, the silvery shields vanished from around them all. And Jarral rose to his feet, blinking.

"For this moment, Jarral," Cryl said, "let your true Talent wake and function, in the full splendour of its power!"

Jarral's eyes snapped wide. His body stiffened, his hands clenched, his hair rippled as if trying to stand on end. And the next tumultuous fragment of a second flung Mephtik's throne room into chaos and catastrophe.

The star-brightness of Flameroc's eyes struck down like a colossal spear of deadliest white heat.

And at the same time something — some *things* — huge but invisible like mighty unseen giants, stormed into the chamber to hurl destruction and ruin before them on every side.

A powerful tremor shook the throne room's floor, heaving up the huge stone slabs as if they were straws. Many of the slabs buckled and split, or thrust up to lean against each other at crazy angles. On the far side of the chamber an immense crack appeared in the floor, running in zig-zag fashion across to the wall. All around the throne room the walls trembled and groaned, with more cracks appearing between the stone blocks. The whole structure cried out in a sound of pain more deep and fearsome than the roar of Flameroc, as dislodged chunks of masonry toppled down in choking clouds of dust.

At the same time the dust was whipped up by a monstrous wind, a gale that whooped through the great doors, ripping them from their hinges as if they were paper. The wind tore the ghastly paintings and tapestries from the walls and shredded them — and as the fragments swirled to the floor, flames erupted from them. Not a molten flame from demonic eyes, but the rich yellow-orange of natural fire. Yet it was fire that seemed uncannily to feed also on masonry dust and bare stone.

The fire hissed and raged as, from no visible source, a torrent of clear water crashed tempestuously down from the terrace, racing along to cascade into the widening crack in the floor, throwing up clouds of mist and steam. Above, in the darkened upper vault of the Tower, more darkness gathered in the form of rolling black clouds. Thunder bellowed from them, as if to echo the groans of the trembling stone, and lightning speared down to blast more splinters from the walls.

The humans had been flung sprawling by the assaults of wind and earthquake. But, by some miracle, none of the falling pieces of masonry, none of the fire or water or lightning, had struck them. Scythe was the first to recover, rising into a half-crouch, surveying the room with his all-round vision.

Not even that vision could fully penetrate the strangling clouds of dust and smoke and steam, but he could see enough. Nearby, Mandra and Archer were dazedly picking themselves up. Farther away, Jarral lay curled in a ball, eyes closed, but seeming unhurt. And nowhere was there any sign of Cryl.

Another explosive tremor shook the stone under Scythe's feet. He sprang away, sword still in hand, and dashed across the chamber, grimly intent. He was looking for Cryl, watching for Flameroc, guarding against falling stone — but his main aim was to complete the task that had brought them to that place.

The thunder rolled again, and he veered aside as lightning smashed down nearby. The floor was humped and uneven, made more treacherous with its trembling and the rubble of fallen stone. Flames leaped around him, dust and steam gathered before him like veils, flung at him by the gale that strove to hurl him from his feet. But he fought through it all, heading single-mindedly towards the steps leading to the terrace.

A few strides more brought him to the edge of the pit — and there he halted briefly, studying the contents of the pit without expression. Some damage showed that a lightning bolt and tumbling chunks of stone had struck down into the pit. But a plentiful number of creatures remained — serpents and lizards and scorpions and spiders of every sort, and some strange varieties of tangled little horrors that did not bear too close inspection. All were in a frenzy at the chaos around them, flailing and threshing, turning on one another, even biting themselves. And many of them in their panic struck again and again at the crumpled, blood-smeared thing that had been the Whiner.

Scythe's face was frozen as he turned away and sprang lightly up the steps of the terrace.

As he reached the top, the Tower seemed to quieten slightly, as if a pause had been declared in that orgy of destruction. To one side Scythe saw the huge wooden throne overturned and smouldering, with no sign of Mephtik. Then he turned to the other side of the terrace — and Flameroc.

Astonishingly, the demon was half-slumped against the wall, skull-head drooping forward. He seemed stunned, helpless, unable to move.

"By all the gods," Scythe said aloud. "It's true. And demons *are* weakened in their presence."

At the sound of his voice Flameroc's head lifted

slightly. Scythe tensed — but the demon's eyes were only a lifeless, dark orange as he looked up dully.

Then the hair lifted on Scythe's neck as he *felt* the power that had arrived. Like a stream of unseen energy, that would make a man tremble with its coldness, and cower from its essence of sheer evil.

Scythe did neither of those things. He merely stood as always, cool and poised and watchful. The icy, unseen power seemed to expand before him. And then it was abruptly gone — and Flameroc had vanished with it.

As if in outrage, the forces of destruction in the chamber renewed their efforts. The wind shrieked at near-hurricane force, lightning raged and stabbed, new flames blossomed from the floor where another quake threw massive stone slabs several feet into the air. The Tower bellowed like a monstrous, dying beast, and more shattered masonry fell in a crushing cascade.

And Scythe turned calmly, having seen the movement behind him.

A ragged, bleeding apparition rose from behind the overturned throne — Prince Mephtik, one whole side of his face scorched and blackened, the other side showing a manic eye and half an insane grin.

"Mephtik is here," he gabbled. "Lightning and fire and earthquake and *nothing* can kill Mephtik I am the prince I have the Blade nothing can kill. . . ." The crazed babble faded as he lurched towards Scythe, clutching in one hand the emerald hilt of the Tainted Blade.

"Blade can kill," Mephtik said. "Slow killing when the full moon rises soon now rises and die from the Blade slow *die*. . . ."

The words leaped upwards into a howl. He raised the Blade high, crouching to spring.

Scythe raised the curved sword — but there was no need. Even through the tumult around him he heard the resonant music of Archer's great bow. The arrow seemed to flower from the Poisoner's wrist, whose howl rose further into an anguished shriek. As the Blade fell from the hand where the arrow jutted, Scythe stepped smoothly forward and caught it in his free hand by the emerald hilt.

Without turning, he could see Archer's broad-shouldered form moving towards the terrace through the storms of smoke and dust.

"Archer!" he yelled. "Get Cryl and the youngsters out! I'll follow you!"

"I cannot find Cryl," Archer shouted mournfully.

"Then get out with Mandra and Jarral!" Scythe yelled. "*Run!*"

Lightning slashed down into the dust clouds, but Scythe had seen that Archer had turned away in time. As a new tremor shook the terrace, splintering two of the broad steps, he became aware that Mephtik was muttering crazily, his one eye staring at the Blade in Scythe's hand. "Don't hurt don't hurt don't hurt don't hurt. . . ."

Then the babble became a whimper as Scythe raised the stained point of the Blade towards the Poisoner's face.

"I could use this on you, Mephtik," he said in a voice thick with hatred. "When the moon rises you would then know the death you have brought to so many."

Mephtik stared at the Blade in glassy silence, dribbling from his ravaged mouth.

"But you might escape that," Scythe went on. "Something might come to your aid, as it came for Flameroc. I want to be sure you're finished."

A burst of fire seemed to walk up into the air nearby, where the dust hung heavy. Mephtik flinched and shivered. Scythe paid no attention.

"I remember the demon's threat to you, Poisoner," he said coldly. "It seems a good idea. Go and seek your own kind, and see which of you is the more venomous."

Dropping both his sword and the Blade, his hands flashed out to grasp Mephtik's ragged robe. Without visible strain, he swung Mephtik off his feet. The Poisoner had only begun a screech of terror as Scythe smoothly pivoted and hurled him from the terrace, a sprawl of skinny arms and legs, into the pit where his monsters threshed.

The screech rose then, agonized and inhuman. But Scythe did not linger to watch. He snatched up both weapons, thrusting the Tainted Blade into the empty sheath at his side that had held the dirk, then sprang down the crumbling steps. In his dash across the chamber floor he had to hurdle a second chasm that had opened among the stones of the floor, duck and twist away from flames that surged up and lightnings that lanced down, battle with all his strength against the gale still howling in through the doors. Yet he reached those doors unharmed.

But there he was nearly driven to his knees by the most deafening roar of all. Catching his balance, he saw behind him an immense weight of stone plunge earthshakingly down. It was the entire high vault of the Tower, in a final thunderous collapse, crashing down into a gigantic heap like a cairn on top of the pit where the Poisoner lay.

Chapter 20

Moments Before Moonrise

"*Elementals*," Mandra said, with awe in her voice.

They were sitting on a dusty hillside just east of the city wall. The darkness around them was lit by scattered stars glinting through light cloud — and by the flames that still leaped here and there among the distant ruins of Mephtik's Tower. Nearby stood the horses that they had taken from the grounds of the Stronghold. No one had tried to halt their flight, though they had passed dozens of dazed and panicky soldiers.

The entire Stronghold had been assaulted by the Elemental forces that had been summoned. As the Tower collapsed, other walls were being tumbled down, other gates blasted open. In the city itself the people either hid in cellars and wailed at this new terror, or stampeded to and fro hysterically on the chaotic streets.

So the four had fled unharmed and had come at last safely to rest on that hillside, finding time to catch their breath, to remember the Tower and to marvel.

"Earthquake and thunderstorm, wind and fire and flood," Mandra was continuing. "All the spirits of the great forces of nature. . . ."

"You could *feel* them there," Archer said, also sounding awed. "Huge . . . Shapeless and invisible, but giants. . . ." She shook her head slowly, remembering. "Their mere presence struck Flameroc down like a reed!"

"Something picked him up," Scythe said dryly. "A stream of evil power. Had to be from the Demon-Driver." His chill smile flashed. "*He'll* have a few things to think about now."

Archer nodded solemnly. "It is no wonder Cryl risked everything for such a Talent. The mightiest of all, which has not been seen in this world for centuries."

Mandra smiled. "And we thought he was just a fire-brand."

Jarral was sitting slightly apart from them, still shirt-less, arms wrapped around his body, staring emptily into the darkness. Now he turned that empty gaze on to the others.

"The full moon is going to rise in a little while," he said hollowly. "And all that Talent and everything won't keep me alive. *Look* at me!"

He let his arms fall away, and once again they all stared at the sickening letter carved on his chest. It was pulsing as furiously as before, and now it had also begun to glow, with a revolting green phosphorescence.

"We can't destroy the Blade without Cryl," Jarral went on. "You've told me that. So I'm going to die at moonrise. There's no Elemental that can keep that from happening."

"Don't give up hope, Jarral," Mandra said gently. "We don't know for certain what happened to Cryl. He might still come to us in time."

Jarral turned bleakly away. "If he's safe, why isn't he here now? And anyway, doesn't he need . . . Urauld, to work magic against the Blade? One way or another, there *is* no hope."

Silence fell, heavy with the helpless sympathy of the others. Slowly Scythe drew the Blade from the sheath at his hip. It also was glowing, with the same evil luminescence as Jarral's wound, which seemed to be taunting their helplessness.

"We have time yet," Archer said. "We could make a fire . . . try to melt the steel. . . ."

Scythe shook his head. "It's a supernatural weapon, Archer. You know that. There's no natural way we can destroy it."

"We could *try*," Archer insisted.

The eerie glow from the wound illuminated the grimace that twisted Jarral's face. "*Try*, then," he said bitterly. He tensed — and a burst of bright flame erupted from the dust in front of Archer.

"Jarral!" Mandra gasped. "You can *control* it!"

"A little," Jarral muttered. "Because of what Cryl did. But I don't have full control."

"That will come when you're . . ." Archer began, but stopped short.

"When I'm grown up?" Jarral finished acidly.

"What about *cold*?" Mandra suddenly said. "Can you call an ice Elemental or something? If the Blade was very cold, it might shatter. . . ."

"I don't know about ice," Jarral said bleakly. "I don't know much about Elementals at all."

"It wouldn't help," Scythe said. "Shattering the Blade wouldn't destroy it. It must *stop existing*. And we can't do that." He slid the evil weapon back into the sheath.

"So we just wait for moonrise," Jarral said with a catch in his voice.

Archer frowned. "No battle is lost until the last blow is struck. There must be *some*thing . . ."

She stopped, startled. Tensely, all four of them rose to their feet, Archer and Scythe gripping their weapons, Mandra and Jarral wide-eyed with puzzlement and fear.

A brightness had come into being at the top of the hill above them.

It was shapeless at first, and cold, like starlight glinting on ice. It seemed to be contained within a frame of unnatural darkness, solid and heavy. And somewhere almost beyond hearing, that darkness held a sound like a wail, as of lost and faceless souls.

Then the solid darkness shifted, shaping itself — and the brightness within it took on form and heat. The four humans stood frozen with horror as the form appeared. Darkly it gathered itself, towering and narrow. The distant wailing rose once more, then died away. The huge shape loomed complete — and from its shadowed face, two pools of molten gold blazed like beacons.

"Flameroc. . . ." Archer breathed.

"Jarral, *do* something!" Mandra said desperately.

But Jarral was standing entirely still, save for the evil pulsing of his wound. His eyes were blank and glassy, reflecting the hot yellow of the demon's glare.

"You will not escape that way now." Flameroc's terrible bass rolled over them. "I have veiled the boy's mind in darkness. He will not use his Talent — ever again. For shortly the full moon will rise."

Scythe stirred slightly, and a tiny tongue of fire licked out from each demonic eye. At once all three of Jarral's companions stiffened as if turned to stone.

"I will keep *you* motionless as well," Flameroc rumbled. "But your minds may remain open, so that you may watch the boy die. Will it interest you to know the manner of that death?"

As the eyes flared again, the three watched in total horror. The luminous, pulsing wound on Jarral's chest began to expand and grow. Slowly, steadily, it spread like a ghastly glowing mould — along his arms, up over his throat, down over his stomach.

And in the wake of that evil glow, as it spread over Jarral's entire body, it left a cracked, blackened, crumbling surface, like flesh seared beyond recognition by fire.

Long moments more, and what had been Jarral was quivering and dying, burnt alive where he stood. Then at last the charred body collapsed, into a pathetically small heap of blackened ash.

Mandra's eyes were screaming, but the outcry was silent in the paralyzing grip of the demon's power. Archer's eyes were also filled with rage and horror — but something else showed briefly in the giant woman's expression. Something thoughtful, calculating. . . .

Flameroc did not notice, for the golden fire of his own eyes was flaring again. And new shock sprang into the expressions of Archer and Mandra, for the small pile of ash had vanished. Jarral was there as before — blank-eyed and motionless, but unharmed.

"That death was an illusion, for your enlightenment," Flameroc rumbled. "The boy's *real* death, in precisely that form, will occur in minutes."

Scythe had shown no reaction to the illusory death. Flameroc's power kept his face and body still, and no expression would ever show in his cold black eyes. But there was an air of great tension coming from him, as if he was straining every grain of his strength to break free. And a similar tension began to grow in Archer, along with the thoughtful look in her eyes.

"Meanwhile," Flameroc was saying, "you may enjoy some further enlightenment. About the fate of that fool of a wizard, Tabbetang."

He paused, the shark-teeth flashing as he savoured the moment.

"As you know," he continued, "the fool dropped his shields in order to summon the boy into the battle. But before the boy's Talent could act, my power had laid hold of Tabbetang. I gathered him up and flung him — towards my Master, whom you irreverently call Demon-Driver."

The thunderous voice deepened even more cavernously. "Your wizard now lies in torment in my Master's palace — where he will remain, undying and agonized, for a hundred years."

The terrible promise rolled away across the hillside, like a final toll of a phantom bell, as Flameroc swept his molten gaze across them all. Yet those eyes did not see a small and furtive movement that began. It was not a hand or a foot or any part of any of the four bodies, still rigidly held by Flameroc's power. It was the hunting knife at Archer's belt. Silently, it slid as if by itself out of its sheath.

Mandra, standing on that side of Archer, glimpsed the movement and fought to conceal the astonishment in her eyes. Scythe, beside Mandra, also saw the knife move with his all-round vision, and the aura of tension and struggle within him seemed to increase.

Flameroc had left their minds awake, in order to torture them by making them watch Jarral die at moonrise. So Archer was able to use her Talent, her mental power, to draw the knife.

And with a final burst of mental strength, the giant woman flung the knife at Flameroc.

The demon's response was one of the most horrible events of that ghastly night. He laughed. He flung up one huge, bony hand to block the knife — letting it stab into and through his narrow palm. And his bass laughter rolled out like a mighty drum, containing an infinity of cruelty.

Dark liquid oozed and dripped from his palm, around Archer's knife, hissing like acid. And the knife drooped and melted, dissolving in that deadly acidity.

"A mortal weapon?" Flameroc asked, through his terrible laughter. "They cannot harm a demon. Did you not learn that facing my vulture? But harm will come to *you*, for your disrespect!"

The molten eyes fixed on Archer, who glared back with stubborn courage. As Scythe hurled maximum effort into his vain struggle, a sudden clear realization flashed across Mandra's face.

She had been surprised by Archer's action, for she would have expected the bow-woman to know that the knife would be useless. But then the realization came. Archer had been trying to *say* something — to *her*.

Had Flameroc been looking, the thought might have been read in her eyes like words.

If Archer can use her Talent, I can use mine.

The thought and the action happened all at once. Within her mind Mandra gathered her Talent, focusing it. It was a Talent that could make people see or not see, that could form clouds upon their minds — or *remove* such clouds.

When Mandra hurled out the power of her Talent, she did not aim it uselessly at the demon. She sent it storming into the mind of Jarral. And it ripped away the veil of darkness from his mind as a high wind tears drapery from a window.

Flameroc whirled, aware of the change, just an instant

away from restoring his grip on Jarral's mind. But that instant was enough. As Jarral burst into full consciousness, he knew without any hesitation what he had to do.

Before Flameroc's eyes could flare, they all heard a faint bubbling splash. And a fountain of bright water spouted up from the earth, directly in front of the demon.

Jarral had wielded his Talent with the new semi-control that being awakened by Cryl had given him. He had summoned an Elemental, a water-spirit. It was not particularly powerful, but power was not needed. In the mere presence of the pure force of a nature spirit, the supernatural power of the demon lost its strength.

The bright fountain, rising no higher than Flameroc's waist, darkened his eyes to a dull orange-red, like guttering candles. He stumbled back, flinching away from the water. And the four humans were suddenly freed rom the paralysis that had gripped them.

Jarral, Mandra and Archer staggered slightly before they caught their balance. Only Scythe stood motionless, still taut, his stony face like an image of cold death as he watched Flameroc flinch away, groaning.

Yet it was only a respite. They all knew that they were safe while the water-Elemental remained, but it would not do so for long. Then Flameroc would be himself again, and would take his vengeance. Nor was there any point in fleeing, for no place would offer sanctuary from the demon's wrath when he recovered.

In that moment Jarral saw that the bright fountain was already beginning to diminish slightly. And then, on the edge of his vision, he saw an equally terrifying sight. A soft brightness was growing in the east as the full moon prepared to lift over the horizon. As he saw it, the pulsing throb of the Blade-wound began to intensify into a burning pain.

He knew he had only seconds to live. Yet the Elemental was still there, though smaller — and Flameroc was still flinching away from it, skull-head drawn back, bone-thin throat arched. . . .

It seemed — familiar. And suddenly the position of the demon, and the pain of his own wound, came together in Jarral's mind. The realization flashed through him like an electric shock. He had seen Flameroc quailing back like that *once before* — on the terrace of Mephtik's throne room.

"Scythe, the *Blade!*" Jarral shrieked. "*The demon fears the Blade!*"

Scythe's response was as swift as a reflex. It was as if his tautened body had been waiting for just that cry. His hand blurred, and the ghastly brightness of the Tainted Blade streaked the night air as it was drawn.

And Scythe threw it with unerring skill, hilt-deep into the heart of Flameroc.

The demon screamed, a sound like the tearing apart of stones, like nameless beasts in the grip of madness. But at once the scream faltered, strangling and bubbling, to become no more than a grinding croak. The Blade seemed to be imparting its glow to the demon. As Flameroc croaked in his agony, the evil luminescence spread to outline and contain his entire towering body.

At the same moment, the dark acid blood that gushed from the wound engulfed the Blade, hissing and crackling.

In seconds the lethal brightness had invaded every part of Flameroc's being. He glowed like a giant, skeletal torch — except for his eyes, which were now a dark and fading red. The glow of his body became more luminous, and for a second all of the demon was transparent, the hillside and the night stars visible in and through his body.

The humans heard a creaking sigh, as if the door to some ageless, forgotten tomb had slowly opened. With it, the last remnants of Flameroc vanished into nothingness.

Even the few drops of his acid blood that had struck the ground disappeared in that final dissolution. Where they had fallen, the ground was deeply scorched. In the midst of the scorch marks, by itself, lay the blackened emerald hilt that had once been fastened to the Tainted Blade.

In the east, the first soft light of the risen moon laid its silver upon the topmost leaves of trees.

And Jarral fell bonelessly to the ground, in a dead faint, where the moonlight cast its glow on the pale, unmarred skin of his chest.

Chapter 21

Southwestwards

Some days later, the four of them were riding through open country to the north-west of Xicanti. They had swung north to find Hob and Pearl, before swiftly putting the city as far as they could behind them. And for once, as far as they knew, they had not been pursued. But none of them had any doubt that, soon enough, pursuit would come.

That thought alone might have been enough to keep Jarral deeply miserable as they rode, even though he had totally recovered from his wound—and from his collapse after all the final, overwhelming horror. Most of the time now he seemed wrapped in sombre thought, looking haunted and haggard. The only time when he seemed to come alive was when he spent a while testing his new-found Talent.

He had still achieved only a small measure of control, so he could summon only small sorts of Elementals — nothing like the cataclysmic forces he had unleashed, with Cryl's help, in the Tower. But even so he used his Talent to some effect, now and then, and not only by lighting campfires. Once, in the farmlands nearer the city, he had let Mandra save her mental strength and had himself called a dust-cloud Elemental to hide the four of them from prying village eyes. Another time, in an arid region, he had called up a flow of sweet spring water. But when the others praised these efforts, he usually scowled and looked displeased.

"It's still too weak," he once said sourly. "I still get real power only when I'm *scared* — like with the yellowjackets or the vulture and those other times. And in the Garden."

Archer nodded. "The stream we thought was an underground river. There was power in plenty. You will find your way to it, Jarral — as you grow to adulthood."

But that merely made Jarral's face tighten and sent him back into his glum withdrawal.

Even Mandra had no luck trying to draw him out of his gloom. In the end it took a remark by Scythe to make it clear what was troubling Jarral, and what could be done about it.

That happened early one morning when the others woke to find Scythe gone from their campsite. But just as they began to grow alarmed, he calmly appeared — with an explanation that was itself alarming.

"I've been keeping watch," he told them. "The Demon-Driver will be sending something against us soon. And it's likely to come in the night."

Archer looked sombre, Jarral turned away with a scowl, and Mandra paled. "What do you think he might . . . send?" she asked.

Scythe shrugged. "Don't ask me how his mind works. If it can still be called a mind."

"He might not send a demon," Archer said. "He will know by now of Jarral's Talent."

"Jarral has to sleep," Scythe said flatly. "So I've been staying awake."

"You can't go on doing that forever," Mandra said.

And those words brought Jarral out of his morose silence. "That's *right*!" he said angrily. "Scythe can't, *none* of us can!" We're just riding along, going nowhere, waiting for something horrible to happen!"

"That is better than what might have been, only days ago," Archer said.

"Is it?" Jarral demanded. "I know, we managed to destroy the Poisoner and a High Demon, and I'm not dying from the Blade now. But you've told me how powerful the Enemy is. He's going to hunt us down, sooner or later. And we don't even have Cryl to help us now!"

Mandra's eyes filled with tears at the mention of the wizard, but Scythe broke in before she could speak. "What do you want us to do, then?" he asked coldly. "Lie down and wait to die?"

Jarral grimaced. "No, of course not. I don't want any of us to die. I just feel . . . so helpless."

"*Help*less?" Mandra said. "You're the least helpless of any of us, with that Talent."

Jarral looked more haunted. "But it's not *enough*. My Talent couldn't save Cryl — and it can't keep us safe now."

Scythe nodded slowly. "That's what bothering you, is it? Blaming yourself because you can't protect us? Jarral lad — one of the worst wastes of energy is fretting about things that can't be done. You have to fix your attention on what *can*. So I'll ask you again — what do you want to do?"

Jarral looked away stonily. "What I want to do is . . . something that can't happen. So I don't know. What *can* we do? Just wait for the Enemy to attack?"

"We could go to my city . . ." Mandra said.

"Or back to the Wellwood . . ." Archer said.

Scythe snorted. "The Demon-Driver will be using all his powers now to find us. Without Cryl, we can't hide."

"And Cryl is a captive," Mandra whispered, "in torment for a hundred years."

"Maybe," Scythe said softly.

Jarral jerked his head up, something wild kindling in his eyes. "What do you mean?"

"What I think *you* meant," Scythe told him, "when you said you want to do something that can't happen."

Archer blinked. "I don't . . ." Then she looked astonished as understanding came to her.

"What are you *saying*?" Mandra asked. "That we should . . . ?" She halted, staring.

Scythe nodded. "Jarral seems to have felt the same, these past days. It sounds suicidal, but it may be all we can do — and what we *should* do. We can't hide from the Demon-Driver, and he'll come after us forever if we run. So. . . ."

"So we go after *him*," Jarral said fiercely, "and try to save Cryl."

An answering fierceness showed in Archer's sudden grin, and Mandra's eyes went wide and bright. "My," she said to Jarral, "you *have* come a long way from the Wellwood!"

Scythe smiled his thin smile. "We might even be safer, at the start, since the Enemy won't expect us to be coming his way. And who knows how far we might get? Some weeks ago we never really thought we could get to Mephtik."

"We had a weapon we didn't know we had," Mandra said, smiling at Jarral.

"And we have it still," Archer said. "A Talent that might help us fight our way to the Enemy's very gate."

"Even if it doesn't," Scythe growled, "I'd rather die fighting than running."

Jarral looked at them calmly. All the gloom and misery that had haunted him for days seemed to have fallen away. "Yes," he said. "I would too."

"But do we even know where to *find* the Enemy?" Mandra asked.

"South-west," Scythe said. "Beyond a mountain range that few humans have ever crossed. We look for a land where the black storm clouds never lift."

Mandra and Jarral shivered slightly, but determination was steel-bright in their eyes, as it was in Archer's. "We will bring some storms of our own to that place, I think," the big bow-woman said.

And, strangely, all four of them were smiling as they mounted their horses and swung them southwestwards.